A Candlelight Ecstasy Romance®

"MY JOB IS ALWAYS ON MY MIND," KATE SAID FIRMLY.

"It is?" Alex buried his hand in her hair and kissed her almost savagely, ignoring her ineffective struggles.

"I *am* going to quit!"

"I'm not," he said, his voice low but emphatic. "I told you, I can separate business from pleasure. You can trust me at the gallery, but in return you have to guarantee to live up to your contract."

"You won't have any reason to complain about my work," she said dryly.

"And you won't have to worry about your employer taking advantage of you—on the job."

"That's the only place I'll be seeing you!"

CANDLELIGHT ECSTASY ROMANCES®

MY KIND OF LOVE

Barbara Andrews

A CANDLELIGHT ECSTASY ROMANCE®

Published by
Dell Publishing Co., Inc.
1 Dag Hammarskjold Plaza
New York, New York 10017

Dell ® TM 681510, Dell Publishing Co., Inc.

Candlelight Ecstasy Romance®, 1,203,540, is a registered
trademark of Dell Publishing Co., Inc., New York, New York.

ISBN: 0-440-16202-5

Printed in the United States of America

First printing—January 1985

To Judy and Chris

To Our Readers:

We have been delighted with your enthusiastic response to Candlelight Ecstasy Romances®, and we thank you for the interest you have shown in this exciting series.

In the upcoming months we will continue to present the distinctive sensuous love stories you have come to expect only from Ecstasy. We look forward to bringing you many more books from your favorite authors and also the very finest work from new authors of contemporary romantic fiction.

As always, we are striving to present the unique, absorbing love stories that you enjoy most—books that are more than ordinary romance.

Your suggestions and comments are always welcome. Please write to us at the address below.

Sincerely,

The Editors
Candlelight Romances
1 Dag Hammarskjold Plaza
New York, New York 10017

CHAPTER ONE

Kate paused before the window, a little breathless even though she'd walked less than ten steps from the taxi. A lone object was on display against a backdrop of forest-green velvet. It was a tea chest veneered with mahogany and satinwood, the masterly workmanship of the Federal period. Although the chest was closed, she knew that the interior was divided into three sections to hold rectangular canisters of tea, a valuable commodity in New York during the early 1800s. Naturally there was no price tag on the piece, and she would have been very surprised if there had been. Gilbert's Antiques Gallery wasn't that kind of shop.

Catching a reflection in the tinted window, she took another minute to make sure she was presentable for the job interview. Her face, not quite round and not exactly heart-shaped, was distorted by the shimmer in the glass; her sun-streaked blond hair was pulled into a severe bun instead of falling casually to her shoulders as it usually did. Twenty-seven years old, with freckles embedded by the Nebraska sun peppering her nose and cheeks, she didn't find it easy to look worldly and experienced. The jacket of her gray pin-striped suit hugged her waist under a narrow belt, which passed muster with its fashionably long lapels; but the startling white of the blouse reminded her of the white collar markings on the family collie. Only one thing encouraged her: She was able to identify the antique in the window.

The only commercial sign on the facade of the building

11

was the discreet gold lettering on the door, which she now opened slowly, not appreciating the melodic chime that announced her arrival. She had hoped to look around the gallery unnoticed, pretending to be a customer for a few minutes, before saying that she had an appointment with Mr. Gilbert. Pulling off the white cotton gloves that moments ago had seemed such a nice touch, she stuffed them into her shoulder bag and stared at the closest object, an elegant sideboard that could have been made by the same craftsman who had designed the tea chest.

"Lovely, isn't it?" a pleasant voice behind her asked. "See how the inner legs are set on a diagonal."

"Yes, that's typical of the New York area, isn't it?" Kate smiled at an older woman whose extreme slenderness was emphasized by a severely cut black dress relieved only by a strand of pearls. With stark white hair falling softly over her brow to one side, she looked distinguished enough to be intimidating, but her expression was warm as they discussed the sideboard as only two lovers of antiques could do.

"I'm not a client," Kate finally admitted, glad she'd remembered not to say "customer." "I'm Kate Bevan. I have an appointment with Mr. Gilbert."

"Nancy Hume." The woman offered her hand. "I'm pleased to meet you, Miss Bevan. Mr. Gilbert is tied up at the moment, but I'll ring his secretary to let her know you're here. Why don't you look around a bit while you're waiting?"

It wasn't an invitation Kate had to hear twice. Wandering slowly down the long, corridorlike length of the salesroom, she was immediately struck by how much it resembled a museum, not the crowded little museum of Americana in Ohio where she'd worked but her idea of an elegant private one. Each piece was displayed in a generous space with none of the crowding that was a trademark of the antiques shops she knew. She recognized hallmarked English silver, an Italian bust, and a Hepplewhite side chair among the artfully displayed treasures. The atmosphere of the place, with its deep blue carpet and recessed lighting, was quiet and subdued. There were no people shopping for antiques this afternoon, but Alex Gilbert wasn't the kind of dealer who depended on drop-in customers. He represented many distinguished private collectors and museums in their quest for fine pieces and ran a thriving import business wholesaling European antiques to the trade. Was she kidding herself to think she might get a job on Fifty-seventh Street in Manhattan dealing in some of the finest pieces that reached the American market? If she was, it was an exciting fantasy and one she had treasured for a long time.

"Mr. Gilbert will see you now." The distinguished-looking woman had come up behind her so quietly Kate was startled. "Go straight back through those doors and up the stairs."

The reception area on the second floor was plush but modern, with thick earth-toned carpeting, beige metal desk and files, and a casual arrangement of side chairs around a low table. The only thing to differentiate it from any other business office was a rather spectacular Art Deco grouping of nubile nudes, their polished metal limbs gracefully arching over a base of gleaming black marble. Here, too, an older woman greeted her.

"Miss Bevan, I'm Blanche Harris." When she smiled her face was a network of tiny wrinkles under crisp copper curls. "Just go right in and Mr. Gilbert will be with you in a moment."

The spacious office was shielded from the outside world by venetian blinds, the narrow strips set between two sheets of glass, and as Kate entered the room she was more than a little uneasy. Remembering the two employees she'd met, she asked herself, Was Alex Gilbert an elderly man who only trusted people over fifty? He was interviewing her for this opening mainly because a friend of her father's had recommended her. Maybe it was only that, a favor to the Chicago antiques dealer who bought wholesale lots from the Gilbert gallery. Perhaps he had no intention of hiring anyone her age.

She forgot her speculations when she looked around the room. An antiques dealer who didn't collect was a rarity, and it reassured her to see that Alex Gilbert wasn't one of them. The three windowless walls were covered with a spectacular collection of posters, the most eye-catching easily recognized as a Toulouse-Lautrec. Crossing the room to study another particularly fine one, a Victor bicycle poster by Will H. Bradley, she smiled at the elaborate floral border and the willowy women cyclists portrayed with frisky black and white swirls and patterns.

"Ms. Bevan?"

"Yes."

She turned and completely forgot her clever little comment about the poster, finding it almost impossible to connect the man in front of her with the dealer who was reputedly one of the most successful in the country. Dark eyes assessed her without reacting in any way, and she felt embarrassed for no reason at all.

"Is something wrong?" he asked politely.

"No, of course not. I'm afraid I expected you to be much older."

"Thirty-four." He smiled. "Would you like to sit here?" He gestured at a cluster of chairs not unlike the ones in the reception area, joining her there instead of sitting behind his desk.

She liked him for that, but his cordiality made her less, not more, comfortable. He was moderately tall, maybe six feet, and slender in a three-piece gray suit with a subdued pattern woven into the fabric. His hair was black, coal-black, and it took her a moment to realize he wasn't handsome in a classical way. His nose was slightly off center; it must have been broken at least once. His brows were dark and thick, and when he smiled his lips curled a little at one corner as

14

though he preferred to test the reaction before committing himself to a broad grin. It was an appealing face, so why was she nervous about meeting his gaze? Sitting rigidly on one of the straight-backed chairs, she gave her skirt a little tug when it slid up over her knees. She wished now that there were a desk between them.

"When I read your resume," he said, getting right down to business, "I was a little surprised you wanted to leave museum work for the grubby side of the business."

Was he teasing? She couldn't be sure, but certainly there was nothing at all grubby about *his* business. A smile was always safe, even though hers was a little tentative.

"I enjoyed working at the museum," she explained, "but I guess I was just born to the trade."

"Your father's a dealer?"

It could have been her mother, but any other reaction would have surprised her. Even though countless women were very successful dealers, men still dominated the upper ranks, and Alex Gilbert was one of the front-runners.

"An auctioneer in Nebraska. I started helping at his estate sales before I was twelve."

He sat back and dropped his hands on his knees, looking totally relaxed and mildly interested. When he didn't say anything, she felt obliged to keep talking.

"I enjoyed my experience at the museum, but I missed the excitement of buying and selling. With the small budget we had, I mostly dealt with donations."

His nails were beautifully manicured, reminding her of the blackened one on her left forefinger, a souvenir of her struggle with a stubborn packing case her last day on the job in Ohio. A benefactor of the museum had donated a cut-glass Libbey punch bowl set—a lovely gift, but there were already two or three similar sets in the basement storage area, with no place to display them. The museum curator's policy was to accept everything, even where there were no-sale strings attached. Kate often thought it was a terrible shame to keep

15

such lovely things in storage. Put on the market, they would find homes with collectors who would use and love them, but the owners often preferred the prestige of having their treasures housed in a museum, even a small one run by a historical society.

"I can understand that." He smiled, and she was relieved not to have to explain. "Your resume also said you took some graduate courses at the University of Delaware."

"Yes. My specialty was Americana, and I took courses on conservation and detecting fakes."

"I always hope my merchandise will move too fast to worry about conservation, but recognizing fakes is vital. My firm guarantees everything we sell to be exactly as represented."

The impact of this was not lost on Kate. In a business where an enormous amount of knowledge was needed just to survive, an unconditional guarantee was invaluable to the buyer.

"Let me show you a photograph," he said, rising to walk to his desk, his movements unhurried but fluid. He picked up a large manila envelope.

The picture he handed her showed two figurines on rather ornate pedestals, clearly oriental with Buddha-like faces. They showed quite a bit of movement for this type of sculpture: the crooked arms were extended and draped garments swirled away from the bodies. She was being tested and knew it, but a glimmer of recognition made her relax and answer calmly.

"They're Japanese bronzes, not very large. Maybe a few inches over a foot." She showed off a little, suggesting a period and value.

"If I'm offered the pair for thirty-two thousand, do you think I should buy them?"

"The easiest way to turn a profit would be to stall the seller while you report them stolen. I believe there's a sizable reward offered for their return." Thank heavens she'd taken time to glance through her trade magazines, even with the hustle of moving to New York. Being alert for stolen merchandise was an ingrained habit.

"Very good."

The full smile he turned on her gave her a warm glow, but she had only reached square one when it came to qualifying for the job. The real issue was whether he thought a young woman would be good for his business.

"I feel like I'm taking an exam, you know."

The spontaneous burst of honesty made him laugh, and his questioning became more a professional discussion than an interrogation.

"I don't know how much you know about my operation," he said after a while. "I see myself primarily as an agent, which means quite a bit of traveling to auctions, sales, and private homes. But a fair share of the profits comes from the wholesale trade. I import container loads from Europe and use my warehouse in Candlebrook as the distributing center."

"That's in Connecticut?"

"Yes. Tell me, what are your living arrangements here?"

"A friend from college was in graduate school at Columbia University. Now she has a grant to study abroad, so I'm subletting her apartment—or maybe I should say her room."

It probably sounded crazy to give up a good job and move to New York just because a friend's studio apartment would be vacant for six months, but he was nice enough not to say so.

"Do I have your phone number?" he asked.

"Yes, it's on my resume."

"You'll hear from me soon, Ms. Bevan."

The hand he extended was warm and hard, grasping hers for several long seconds, making her wonder if she would ever see him again. His courtesy in interviewing a customer's friend's daughter could take her only so far. Maybe, being

17

himself so young to be at the top of his profession, he liked to add dignity to his firm by employing older people. If so, she was finished before she started.

She was in the street before the reaction set in. If her pulse was fluttering, it was only because Alex Gilbert was unlike any of the other men she'd met in the trade. Summers during college and after graduation she had worked antiques shows, selling her own merchandise and meeting hundreds of other dealers in the Midwest and Southwest. Many of the men had retired from another occupation or were selling antiques as a sideline; some, especially the younger ones with bushy beards, cowboy hats, or even outdated hippie ponytails, dreamed of getting rich on baseball cards, beer cans, or Elvis Presley memorabilia. The minority, those canny businessmen who were knowledgeable and successful, ran more to paunches and balding heads. She had never been tempted to become involved with a fellow dealer. It stunned her that she couldn't stop thinking about the appealing man who had just interviewed her.

You wanted to play in the major leagues, she reminded herself, still standing outside the gallery, not quite ready to come to grips with the problem of getting home. Stepping into a world where people bought and sold Queen Anne armchairs, Winslow silver, and Chippendale highboys— things she had seen only in books in Nebraska—had been her dream for years. Alex Gilbert was the kind of man who was comfortable in this world: sophisticated, intelligent, elegant, witty, certainly attractive to women clients. But did she belong there? Her minor triumph in identifying the stolen bronzes didn't seem important enough to gain her entry into his business; she had only done what was expected of any experienced dealer. Slowly, without paying attention to the midafternoon bustle of traffic, she started walking toward what she hoped was the right bus stop.

I'm not even sure I can survive here, she thought dejectedly. The subway was the quickest way back to her tiny borrowed apartment, but she was not yet ready to tackle its puzzling depths. She couldn't even remember which bus to take. What she needed was funny animals painted on the vehicles like those on some rural school buses: a panda for Eighty-first Street, an alligator for Greenwich Village, a honey bear for Broadway. She stopped for a moment before another antiques store to look at the merchandise crammed into the windows on either side of the door. Of the fifty or more items haphazardly arranged there, there wasn't one she couldn't identify and price, but what good was it to be so darn smart if she couldn't feel comfortable with high-society buyers?

Turning in what she hoped was the right direction, she walked with a briskness she didn't feel, hardly noticing the warm, if gritty, spring wind. Untangling her foot from a loose sheet of newsprint, she wondered if anyone would stop if she sat down on the pavement and howled.

By the time she'd bought groceries and carried a heavy bag up to her third-floor apartment, she'd convinced herself Gilbert's Antiques Gallery would send a polite form letter thanking her for her interest, and that would be the end of it. Money wasn't an immediate problem, thanks to the skillful buying and selling she had done before taking the museum job; but finding the kind of position she wanted was going to be tough. The auction houses were her best prospects if she didn't want to return to museum work; but the large ones would, at best, pigeonhole her as an expert on American folk art, which she was, and have her spend all her time apprais-ing quilts, weather vanes, and samplers. She wanted the ex-citement of buying and selling with the high rollers, and the woman in her knew she could handle it. It was the little girl from Butterfield, Nebraska, who wasn't sure she could mix successfully with sophisticated clients.

Her most immediate problem, however, was the refrigera-tor; she couldn't bring herself to put fresh cartons of yogurt, orange juice, and eggs into an appliance whose interior was

19

coated with last Christmas's solidified eggnog. She was almost grateful that Linda had left a few challenges to take her mind off Alex Gilbert, and when the phone rang shortly after six, she was still elbow-deep in sudsy wash water, finishing off the top of the almost-miniature gas stove in the small alcove that served as a kitchen. Her mother must have waited until five o'clock Nebraska time, when the phone rates went down, before placing her call.

"Ms. Bevan?"

"Yes." A little bubble in her throat made her voice sound squeaky; she hadn't expected the coup de grace so soon.

"Alex Gilbert. Did I mention that the job isn't a nine-to-five one?"

"No, I don't think you did."

"There's a party tonight I'd like you to attend."

"Officially—I mean, as your representative?" She was too nervous to be sure whether he was offering her a job.

"Not exactly. Can you be ready by seven?"

She glanced down at her faded jeans, calculated how long it would take to shampoo and dry her hair, and knew it would be impossible.

"Yes," she heard herself saying. "How will I get there?"

"I'll come for you."

He hung up abruptly, and she still wasn't sure if she was being hired or dated. Maybe this was another test, like identifying the stolen bronzes. He wanted to see how poised she was in a social situation. Probably he spent more time at parties than at his gallery, making contacts, getting to know the right people, charming potential buyers.

Holding the hair dryer over her head with one hand and, with the other, trying to apply a foundation that would mute her freckles, she mentally sorted through the contents of the closet. What on earth would she wear? Her little basic black dress was usually a safe choice, but Nancy Hume wore one not unlike it to clerk in the Gilbert gallery. Some impression

20

she would make on Alex wearing hers to a party! And when did she start thinking of him as Alex?

Giving her hair a few careless tosses to make it dry faster, then reaching for her lip brush, she managed to touch the back of her neck with the hot metal rim of her old dryer, burning the sensitive skin. A little first-aid cream took away most of the pain, but applying it slowed her down. Worse, she undoubtedly had a red mark in a very noticeable place; she would have to wear her hair down to cover it, so good-bye to sophistication!

Her clothes were hanging in a jumble of plastic, stuffed into suit bags she had borrowed from her father for the move. The contents of those bags could only be seen through a small transparent window. The clothes weren't even sorted by seasons, and she had to prod her memory just to remember what the weather was. She could wear the same spring suit that she'd worn to the interview, but wouldn't he think she was gauche wearing a daytime outfit to a party? After unzipping three bags and pawing through them, she settled for a Wedgwood-blue jersey with little ruffled sleeves and a full, swirly skirt, remembering too late that the only shoes that went with it were skimpy summer ones. Was it too early for white shoes? The time for making choices was gone; the shoes were on her feet before she realized her white purse was somewhere in the yet-to-be-unpacked cartons, and the charcoal one she'd been carrying looked awful with her outfit.

The buzzer sounded, and she felt absolutely idiotic talking to someone she couldn't see.

"Alex Gilbert," he announced nonchalantly.

"I'm all ready. I'll come right down." This wasn't exactly true, but how could she finish her hair, put on her belt, and find her apartment key while he stood staring at the gray cleaning water she'd forgotten to drain from the sink?

"It looks like rain," he said, less helpfully than intended. Did he think her apartment didn't have a window? He

21

wasn't far from wrong! The one lace-covered rectangle showed only the bleak brownish front of an apartment building not unlike hers. She could only see the sky when her nose was two inches from the glass, but during her Nebraska childhood she'd seen enough horizon to last a long time.

"Thank you. I'll be right down."

Too late she remembered her intention to take the beige-colored raincoat to the cleaners. A big, noticeable black smudge under the right pocket almost made her leave it behind, but her umbrella was somewhere in a corrugated cardboard box along with her paperweight collection and a dozen or so copies of *Vogue* from the 1930s. A born collector, she'd sent twenty or so cartons of her belongings to her parents' home in Butterfield before coming to New York. But even that shipment hadn't reduced her possessions to an amount manageable in a studio apartment. A quick check in the full-length mirror on the bathroom door showed that her purse would cover the spot if she held it at just the right angle.

How could she get out of breath going downstairs? Alex was waiting in the utilitarian, tiled foyer, reading the names on each of the tarnished bronze mailboxes.

"Sorry to keep you waiting," she said.

"There's no rush except I'm illegally parked."

He took her arm and rushed her down the short flight of steps to the pavement. She had expected a Jaguar or a Mercedes or even a Ferrari: the station wagon showed a practical streak she appreciated. What dealer with a head for business would drive a vehicle too small to hold a lowboy or a secretary?

"No ticket this time." He smiled forgiveness and opened the door for her, then got in behind the wheel.

"I didn't expect to hear from you so soon," she said.

"Snap decisions are my specialty."

Had he decided to hire her? Though still uncertain, she had little time to worry about it as he zipped through traffic, changing lanes, slipping in front of taxis, and stopping only inches from other car bumpers. That in New York everyone drove that way tempered her irritation somewhat and made her glad she'd sold the lumbering old van that had served her so well for hauling merchandise to antiques shows. She'd driven across the Rockies and through the deserts of the Southwest by herself, but was darned if she would attempt to drive across Manhattan.

"I forgot all about this party until a few minutes before I called you. Have you had dinner?"

"No."

"Me neither. If the prospects of eating there aren't good, we'll cut out early. I did want you to meet a Persian rug dealer."

"A friend?"

The question seemed to surprise him. "We sometimes do business."

Even in her part of the woods dealers often bought cooperatively. A specialist in glass and china might pick up a beautiful pine dry sink or pie safe at a bargain price and sell it for a very small markup to a friend who specialized in country furniture, expecting a return of the favor someday. Finding quality antiques at prices that allowed a profitable return was always the dealer's biggest problem. Fine, reasonably priced antiques practically sold themselves.

Alex parked in an underground garage that she hadn't even noticed from the street, then ushered her out of the low-ceilinged cavern with one hand under her elbow. An elevator deposited them in a lobby with pinkish veined marble walls and a terrazzo floor, and another carried them to the fourteenth floor with accompanying creaks and groans.

"Do you live here?" she asked.

"No, this is where the party is."

"The garage doesn't look like a public one."

"No. Karazan doesn't have a car, so he told me to use his place."

She felt naive trying to fathom the transportation problems of New York City, but she wasn't going to feel at home until mobility seemed less of a bugaboo.

The apartment they entered without knocking seemed to be short on oxygen, the sweet, pungent smokiness of incense so cloying she couldn't imagine how anyone could enjoy it. The bare floor was of highly polished wood stained an earthen red, but the walls were covered with rugs, brilliantly colored and intricately patterned. Instead of chairs, low divans stood out from the walls, and giant red and deep blue cushions were scattered everywhere, a few of them occupied by guests too intent on their conversations to notice the new arrivals.

"Through here," Alex said, parting jangling strips of beads to enter a much larger and more crowded version of the first room.

"Is this his home or his shop?" she whispered, more than a little awed by the setting and the guests.

A woman in a shimmering silver gown that plunged to her navel smiled at Alex with scarlet lips and greeted him by name; she then resumed conversation with a stout man wearing loose yellow trousers, much like harem pants, that were tightly gathered at his thick ankles. His black embroidered felt slippers actually curled up at the toes, and his only garment on top was a vest that matched the footwear.

"Omar lives here, but he's never reluctant to sell a rug off the wall."

Alex found their host in a third room where guests were already sampling an assortment of exotic foods laid out on long tables covered with purple linen cloths. Silver serving platters sat beside an ornately incised samovar that looked more Russian than Persian, and the aroma of strong Turkish coffee and highly spiced lamb overcame the lingering scent of incense.

Kate found Omar Karazan something of a disappointment after seeing his exotic home. Short and balding, he wore a smartly tailored black business suit and a narrow gray tie. Nodding his head to acknowledge Alex's introduction, he quickly jumped into a discussion of an oriental auction that had fallen short of his expectations. Alex interrupted the tirade to ask Kate if he could take her coat, but their host rather impatiently indicated a door on the far side of the room where she would find a place to leave it.

Feeling dismissed and awkward, she followed a narrow corridor to a bedroom where a few other coats were lying on a black plush bedspread embroidered with a hundred shades of purple, red, and pink silk thread. The surface swayed when she tossed her raincoat and purse on it, and she couldn't resist prodding it to watch the water-filled mattress jiggle again. Returning to the party, she felt like a very plain Alice in a very exotic wonderland. Alex and the host were nowhere in sight, and no one seemed to notice her. She wandered through all three rooms, mostly seeing the backs of guests engaged in loud, laugh-filled conversations. The man in yellow harem pants made a halfhearted attempt to flirt with her, but the powerful garlic fumes he sent her way made his departure a relief. Holding court in the larger of the two rooms, which was furnished mostly with pillows, was a sleek-looking woman of indeterminate age. Her green-sequined miniskirt hugged prominent hipbones, and white hose accentuated the bizarre thinness of her legs. Kate recognized her from somewhere but didn't have enough nerve to eavesdrop on her conversation. Why on earth had Alex brought her here? She felt like a weed among rare orchids and Venus's-flytraps. It wasn't surprising that no one seemed to see her.

A few tentative notes from a stringed instrument reached her ears over the din of conversation. Moving toward the source, she came upon a knot of people at the beaded doorway which blocked her way for a few moments, then she found herself part of a crowd gravitating toward the soft melodic tones of some unidentifiable instrument. Before reaching a spot where she could see, she heard a fine tenor voice singing a ballad to the low strumming. Alex, now in his shirt sleeves, was sitting on a low stool, his long legs stretched out and his head bent in concentration over a mandolin, the honeyed patina of the wood gleaming as he skillfully plucked the metal strings with a plectrum.

> "A love that dies when first to bud,
> Was e'er a maid so heartless as she?"

He looked up, running his eyes over the hushed crowd until he met her gaze; then he continued his soft singing:

> "Oh, Katie, my love, I would I could woo you,
> Oh, Katie, my love, I would I could woo you."

He smiled directly at her, and she suspected there was no Katie in the original version of the ballad. People who only minutes before had seemed blasé and wrapped up in themselves were now applauding him warmly and urging him to continue. From a lively ballad about the king's men taking poor old Paddy, he went on to a bittersweet lament for love long lost. She was embarrassed by the tears that filmed her eyes, and disturbed by the way she felt. It was a relief when Alex handed the instrument to his host and slipped into his suit jacket. A few more songs like the last one and she would imagine she was in love with the singer! Nothing could be more complicated than a crush on her new boss—if he was in fact offering her the job.

Several people waylaid him, including the woman in the silver gown who was enthusiastically praising his performance. Kate backed away from them until a pillow-stacked divan blocked her retreat, not wanting to intrude when praise was being heaped on him.

He's tired, she thought, noticing the dark shadows under his eyes as he talked and laughed with a growing circle of

26

admirers. She felt guilty because she wanted to comfort him. Next she would be telling him to get more rest or making chicken soup for him. Maybe the incense had gone to her head.

He rejoined her, finally, suggesting she collect her coat so they could leave.

"Wouldn't you like to eat?" she asked. It seemed an awful shame to pass up the stuffed grape leaves and the intriguing rice dish, not to mention the array of unusual fruits and cheeses. She'd always wanted to taste goat cheese.

"I'm faint with hunger," he whispered close to her ear, "but darned if I'll bite into a sheep's eye."

They left after a word of thanks to the host and, in Kate's case, a final wistful glance at the buffet table. Had she had a little more nerve, she would have wrapped a piece of a silvery-looking confection in a napkin and spirited it away in her purse. There was nothing, with the possible exception of rattlesnake meat, that she wouldn't try once, and one of the delights of moving to New York City was the opportunity to sample gourmet treats from every corner of the world. Nebraska had the best steaks in the world, but she would take broiled swordfish or linguine with clam sauce any day. Her grocery budget always allowed for one spectacular meal a week, even if it meant six days of boiled eggs and salad.

"I take it you're not a gourmet," she teased in the elevator.

He smiled sheepishly.

"Definitely not! I even prefer California wine to French."

He took her to a cozy little restaurant whose only pretension was a red awning over the six iron-railed steps that descended to the entrance. The menu was simple: seven cuts of steak and, for variety, ground steak. She ordered a six-ounce filet mignon guaranteed to come from Omaha.

"Your ballads were lovely," she said. They were both relaxed now and deciding whether the last few bites were worth the effort. "Is that mandolin very old?"

27

"Not as old as Omar would have me believe, but it's Italian and well made. If he comes down quite a bit, I may buy it for my collection."

"You collect musical instruments?"

"Only stringed instruments. Guitars, ukuleles, banjos. Have you ever heard a balalaika?"

"I'm afraid I don't even know what it is."

"A sort of Russian guitar. Mine has gut strings and is plucked by hand, although professional players are using wire strings and a leather pick."

"Do you sell many musical instruments?"

"Not enough to worry about. Unless I pick up something showy like a harp or a harpsichord, I rarely handle them. I like to keep business and pleasure separate."

Was this evening business or pleasure? She was dying to know if the job was hers for sure, but part of her hoped he enjoyed her company too. Much as she wanted to work for Alex—and he was officially Alex now—a purely professional relationship wasn't going to be easy.

He tried to stifle a yawn, but she caught him at it.

"It's not the company," he said, beguiling her with his lopsided grin. "It's the long hours, which is why I need an assistant right away. My last one left to go into business for himself."

Holding her breath without realizing it, she waited in agonized suspense.

"Can we discuss salary, benefits, hours—that kind of thing—in the morning?" he asked.

"I have the job, then?" She felt limp with relief; the only thing worse than not being hired would be not seeing him again.

"Did you really doubt it?" His eyes, in spite of the shadows of fatigue, sparkled with mischief and something else.

"You weren't very specific."

"A bad habit. The first thing you'll have to learn is how to read my mind."

28

"Are you sure you want me to do that?" The signals she could read were definitely unsettling to a new employee, but she couldn't resist flirting a little.

"Maybe not just yet."

Of course he didn't kiss her good night. She probably only imagined that he wanted to. As she set the alarm to rouse her early for work, she wondered if "Oh, Katie, My Love" was an authentic folk ballad.

CHAPTER TWO

Skirt or slacks, slacks or skirt? Kate debated with herself as she went about her early-morning routine. She much preferred slacks, especially if the day's work involved stooping and bending to inspect larger antiques; but the two female employees she'd met at the gallery had been wearing dresses. Maybe Alex expected the women in his firm to dress formally.

Her new job probably didn't involve working with hammer or crowbar, so she decided on a flared lightweight camel-colored wool skirt and a tailored beige silk blouse. She placed around her neck a butternut with a little carved face, her lucky piece, because she needed all the help possible for this big first day on East Fifty-seventh Street.

Blanche Harris was near at hand to let her in through the private entrance in the rear.

"Mr. Gilbert isn't here yet, so why don't you have a good look around. The gallery won't be open for another hour."

Did his employees call him Mr. Gilbert in private? She made a mental note not to use his first name at work until she knew if the others did.

Looking around alone was no chore. The receiving room was a model of efficiency in spite of the cluttered look that went hand in hand with back rooms in the antiques business. A quiet, burly man with a gray crewcut introduced himself as Jack Fisher. He did not explain his position in the firm, but his workingman's uniform, of dull green with the gallery

30

name on the shirt pocket, suggested he was in charge of moving merchandise in and out. She left him after exchanging a few words about the gloomy weather; it was more prudent, she decided, to let Alex define her role in the business before she questioned others about their responsibilities.

The third floor, reached by stairs and by a slow-moving freight elevator, was an antiques lover's paradise. Alex's library was housed here in a large open work area with tables and benches for appraisals and minor repair work. Rust-colored industrial carpeting covered the floor, and the walls were almost completely covered with shelving and odd hanging objects: picture frames, tools, measuring equipment —the paraphernalia of the business. One bench accommodated a black light, indispensable in detecting repairs and flaws in china, paintings, and other objects, while another was devoted entirely to polishing pastes and equipment. Except for a small kitchen-lounge, a restroom, and a photography darkroom, the whole floor was one large work area. Kate anticipated spending many long, satisfying hours there; as Alex's assistant she wouldn't be expected to work in the public gallery except for special showings.

"Having a good look?" Alex had come up the stairs so quietly that she hadn't heard him.

"Yes, you're certainly well equipped up here. I didn't realize John Risk has a new book out on Russian glass." She commented on the first thing she could think of.

"It's not in the stores yet. He sent me a copy. I sold him several of the pieces illustrated."

He opened a quarto-size book and pointed to a color picture of a beaker ornately decorated with gold. "It was a coup getting this piece. Made at the imperial factory around 1750. Those are the initials of the czarina between the gilded vine scrolls."

She looked at the page but all she saw was his hand, lean and darker than hers, the skin tight over prominent knuckles. How would those fingers feel on her skin, caressing her cheek, flicking over the hollow of her neck? She gave herself a mental kick and forced her attention to the illustration of a hundred-year-old green wineglass decorated with silver.

Did he realize she wasn't concentrating on the illustrations in the book? She quickly mumbled some appreciative words. Working here was the opportunity of a lifetime; she simply could not blow it by letting her new boss bedazzle her.

"Have you worked with computers?" he asked.

"My father is just beginning to use one for some of his business. He gave me a few lessons when I went home for Christmas, but I'm only a beginner."

"So am I, but let me show you Lizzie anyway."

"Lizzie?"

"I think of her as the tin Lizzie of the computer age. All I ask is that she putts along at her own slow pace when I crank her up."

The computer was housed in a second-floor room along with a copying machine and several files. Kate sincerely hoped her job would keep her on the third floor. She had an absolute horror of punching the wrong key and losing the total bank of information stored in a cold, impersonal machine, even though her father had assured her that the chance of making such an error was not great.

"The real key to my business is knowing who wants what," Alex said after showing her a few basics. "The computer holds descriptions of every piece in my inventory, here and in Candlebrook, but out in the field we have to rely on memory to guess whether a collector will want a piece being offered for sale. My file goes back to day one in this location, and your first job is to study it."

He pulled out a metal drawer housing a long row of cards. "The top drawers contain clients' names with past sales and current needs. The lower ones contain want lists and collecting interests categorized that way. Begin with them." He took out a white lined card. "For example, Mr. and Mrs.

George Paxton. In 1979 they bought a New England tea table and in 1980 a pine breakfront, but they were furnishing a house in Westchester then. Now they rarely buy furniture, but show them a quality cut-glass biscuit box with silver mounts and lid, and it's almost a sure sale."

She was frowning at the tremendous task of memorizing his clients' interests. "Are they on your computer too?"

"No, I debated whether they should be, but I only want one copy of each entry available. No loose computer copies floating around. If you borrow a card for reference, make sure it's back in the file the same day."

This was reasonable, she knew. A competitor would find a list of his carefully cultivated clientele a gold mine. "It always fascinates me to read what people collect."

"What do you collect?" he asked.

"How do you know I do?" It was a silly question considering her profession.

"Who doesn't?" he teased.

No one in his world, the world she wanted to enter.

"Paperweights, but mine aren't the expensive French and American, mostly just advertising ones, the kind given away after the 1880s. Oh, and I save early fashion magazines too. And hand-carved whatnots."

"Whatnots?"

"You know, balls carved inside of balls inside of balls— that sort of whittlers' art."

"Very foresighted."

Why did he smile at her that way when she was trying so hard to concentrate on the challenges of her new job?

"So is collecting posters," she said, "if you started soon enough."

"I did. My first one was a circus poster I begged from a neighborhood grocer when I was about ten."

"You were an early starter." So was she.

"I was the pampered only son of two fanatical collectors. My mother had a business importing jewelry, and my father

33

worked for an airline. They're retired now, but both traveled constantly and dragged home everything from monkey skins to cowbells."

"It sounds like an exciting childhood." She thought of the hundreds of Nebraska farms where her father had held auctions, unable to sort one from another in her memory: neat frame houses and barns against a stark panorama of wheat or corn fields.

"When Mother wasn't dragging me off to Taiwan to look at gemstones, my father was pulling rank to get family rates to fly to Hong Kong or Brazil. I went to Yale to get off the merry-go-round and found I could hardly wait to get back on."

Her sigh held a combination of envy and awe; until she'd listened to him, her childhood—a time of hanging around auctions and spending her few dollars on exciting little treasures—had seemed uncommonly satisfying. She wouldn't have traded it for any other way of growing up, but his life-style did make hers seem commonplace.

He was looking at her closely, his expression that of a connoisseur admiring a work of art. Looking up from the card drawer and meeting his gaze, she felt exposed and vulnerable, welcoming his assessment but more than a little afraid of it. Life was going to be complicated enough proving she was worthy of the job; she didn't know how to cope with the look of promise in his eyes.

"I'd like to give you a week just to learn the stock and my clients' needs," he said regretfully, "but we're really swamped around here. I'm supposed to appraise things people are bringing to a charity show this afternoon. Do you think you could handle that so I can look at a tall-case clock on Park Avenue?"

"Sure," she said, hoping her voice was brimming with self-confidence. "Where is it?"

"A church social hall. I'll have to look up the address. Just jot down the taxi expenses and turn them in to Blanche.

Damn, we haven't even talked salary, have we." He glanced at his watch. "Look, I have an appointment in less than ten minutes. You'll only have to stay at the show until five. Would you mind meeting me here afterward?"

"No, not at all. Am I supposed to give retail appraisals? Do you want me to try to buy better pieces?"

"Working this show is just a goodwill mission. A friend of mine is the chairperson. Probably all you'll see will be Victorian doodads, so just give the owners a rough idea of what things are selling for. If something nice does turn up, give the owner my card and let him know we may be interested."

Somewhere in the rush of getting to the antiques show, she forgot lunch. Blaming the churning in her stomach on hunger, she tried to talk herself out of being nervous. After all, this sounded like a minor event compared with the big shows in Des Moines or Dallas or Houston, and she had set up at all of them. It was only the jolting ride in the cab and the strangeness of the city that were undermining her confidence.

Liar, she accused herself, ruthlessly cutting through her puny excuses. Don't think about meeting Alex after five o'clock, and the appraisals will be a breeze.

The room was more crowded than dealers liked, with aisles barely wide enough to accommodate the viewers, but it looked like home to Kate. The women at the admission table greeted her enthusiastically, and one introduced her to the chairperson, Mrs. Webster. A willowy platinum blonde who towered over Kate's five and a half feet, she obviously wasn't thrilled about the substitution.

"Alex will be along later?" she asked after withdrawing her long, cold fingers from Kate's hand.

"I'm terribly sorry. He said he'd be unable to make it this afternoon."

The chairperson frowned, her forehead creasing in deep lines that makeup couldn't disguise, and Kate wasn't the least bit sorry about Alex's absence.

"Well, I'll see him next Saturday." Mrs. Webster sounded just a little smug about that.

People weren't exactly lined up by the sign that read Appraisals by Gilbert's Antiques Gallery, but several were hovering near the easel holding the announcement. A few others were near the roped-off area, and all were clutching bundles or paper sacks containing the treasures they wanted appraised. The afternoon promised to be a busy one, which was fine with Kate. The more her mind was on business, the less she would think about Alex. She hadn't given up a placid, pleasurable life in Ohio to get herself into an emotional tangle over any man. Once she had been tempted to give up her dreams for settled domesticity in a small Nebraska town. The summer before starting college had been one of feverish love and agonizing decisions. She'd loved Randy and tried to prove it in every possible way, but she hadn't been able to do the one thing he demanded: forget her own plans and marry him right away. Angry and hurt, he'd vowed it was all over between them if she went to the University of Nebraska. Sometimes, in melancholy moments, his rejection still stung.

With no way of telling who had been waiting the longest, she stepped behind a table and made a production out of taking off and folding her coat—letting a line form as she did so. The first person was a frail little woman with wispy white hair that showed her pink scalp. She might have been someone's sweet old granny, but her eyes gave her away. Pale and bulging, they were sizing up Kate; disapproval showed in the deep lines on either side of the woman's tiny puckered mouth.

"Supposed to be a man comin' to say what things're worth," she complained.

"Mr. Gilbert wasn't able to be here, but I'm a fully qualified appraiser. How may I help you?"

"Is he comin' later?"

"No, I'm afraid not."

36

"Well, I'm thinkin' of sellin' this."

"Let's have a look," Kate urged with patience born of long practice.

"My mother had this doll when she was little."

After one more shrewdly appraising look the woman extracted a doll from a wrinkled paper bag, handing it to Kate as if it were the crown jewels. It was definitely old; the composition head was crazed with hundreds of minute lines.

"It's got these here letters on the neck." The nail that pointed to the smudgy marking was almost as gray as the two dingy teeth in the doll's open mouth. "What'll you pay for it?"

Kate could make out a *J* and a *K* with an unreadable smudge between them and knew the old woman wanted her to believe it was a Kestner doll, which would be worth hundreds of dollars if in fine condition. This doll was neither fine nor Kestner. The mark was such an obvious forgery that Kate wanted to smile. The body parts looked like rejects from a doll hospital. The feet didn't match, and one hand lacked tips on all its fingers. At the most the doll might bring ten dollars from a sentimental collector at a flea market.

"It would be such a shame to sell a family heirloom," Kate said. "I can imagine how you must treasure a doll your mother played with. The ten dollars or so it would bring wouldn't begin to compensate for the loss of it."

The woman had hoped for a male appraiser, thinking he would be less knowledgeable about dolls and so would make her a good offer based on the obviously phony mark. If that doll had been in the woman's possession more than a year, Kate would eat it. The white-haired little lady was a picker, a person who haunted thrift shops, flea markets, rummage sales, and other junk outlets, buying solely to resell. The doll probably cost her a dollar at the most. She hoped to con someone into paying a big price for it, but only a naive, inexperienced dealer or collector would fall for the "mother" bit.

37

"Ten dollars!" Her voice was squeaky with indignation. "I'd never sell it for that. It should be worth fifty."

"Our firm doesn't deal in dolls," Kate explained, conscious of the line of waiting people, "so that was only my estimate of its value, not an offer to buy."

The woman jammed the poor dilapidated toy into the bag and stalked off to try some of the other dealers. By the end of the day she would probably be glad to settle for five dollars, Kate suspected.

It was a pleasure to tell the next person her scenic blue and white Staffordshire plate dated from the early 1800s and was worth more than eight hundred dollars.

"Imagine," the flabbergasted inquirer said, "my grandmother used it as a bread plate." She carried it away as though the pressure of her fingers might shatter it.

Kate thoroughly enjoyed having her expertise put to the test, and she wasn't embarrassed to take the information of a man who had brought a large three-liter Mettlach stein, an outstanding example with a Heidelberg scene. With prices going into the thousands, she wanted to check a price guide to ensure accuracy. The man was very appreciative, especially since he wasn't aware that prices had gone so high.

"Can I pay you?" he asked, handing her a business card showing he was a paper-goods salesman.

"Ordinarily appraisals can cost up to ten percent of the value of the item, but Mr. Gilbert is donating my services today."

"Then I'll be sure to make a donation to the show's charity when I leave," he said, thanking her again.

Why had Alex agreed to offer free appraisals? Was it sweet charity on his part, or was it a very personal favor to the show's chairperson? She couldn't forget Mrs. Webster's comment about seeing him Saturday. Wondering about it took the edge off her pleasure when she gave estimates that pleased the owners. How could she possibly be jealous of a man she had met only yesterday? It was absurd, and she'd better not catch herself humming "Oh, Katie, My Love" another time!

The man now standing in front of her was different. Kate sensed it immediately, even though she couldn't give a single logical reason for suspecting him. He was casually but neatly dressed, very average-looking in every way and with a trace of an accent, possibly British or maybe Canadian.

"My wife's aunt died a while ago," he said, slowly freeing a table lamp from a box filled with packing pellets. "She had a houseful of this old stuff, and we'd like to sell the lot to a reputable dealer."

The lamp with a shade of leaded green and amber flowers was lovely. Easily identifying it as very desirable early 1900s art glass made by Philip Handel in New York City, she was sure Alex would be interested in merchandise of this quality. She let the man talk while she pretended to examine the lamp base.

"She was an eccentric old lady—regular junk collector. We don't want to muck around with auctions and such. Just want a reasonable offer on the lot. Got it all loaded in our van if you'd like to look it over."

He went on and on, regaling her with stories of his aunt's foolish miserly ways, until Kate knew her first impression was right. He was trying to unload a vanful of hot antiques.

"Mr. Gilbert would have to see it. I'm not authorized to purchase large lots."

"I thought that's why you're here." His voice remained pleasant, if just slightly challenging, but his eyes narrowed in annoyance.

"I can make an appointment for you at the gallery at your convenience. If your other pieces are of the same quality as this lamp, we'll be very interested."

"No, that's not possible. We're on our way to Toronto. I was hoping to unload the lot and go. What about the lamp? I wouldn't say no to an offer on that."

She suggested a price so close to the retail value that he

looked like a man who had won the lottery. Reaching for her purse, she took out her checkbook, knowing her current checking balance wouldn't cover the amount she'd offered for the lamp.

"Do you have a business card and a driver's license?" she asked.

"A Canadian license. Will that do?"

She carefully wrote the check, then put his license information on a pad of paper and stalled until she spotted one of the security guards at the end of the aisle. The would-be seller was a pro; he saw her eyes give the signal.

"Before I accept your check, I'd better make sure it's okay with my wife." He picked up the lamp, ignoring the check she was pressing on him.

"It's a more-than-fair offer," she said persuasively.

"I'll be right back." He abandoned the box and packing, briskly carrying the lamp away.

The guard hesitated a moment too long when she rushed up to explain her suspicions. The man with the lamp had disappeared into a corridor leading to the men's rest room; apparently he had scouted for emergency exits before attempting to unload his merchandise. The van, if there was one, disappeared as smoothly as the man. All Kate could do was tear up her useless check. Had he accepted it, she could have made a fuss about the lamp being a fake and demanded proof of ownership. She needed more than vague suspicions to call the police, however much he'd confirmed them by running away. All she could do now was give his driver's license information to the police, and it was probably a fake.

The show would last through the weekend, but her stint would end at five o'clock. Hungry and discouraged, she didn't at all relish reporting the day's activities to Alex. As a legitimate dealer, he had to hate thieves as much as she did. Anyone purchasing stolen antiques could lose in every way. The thief got away with the money, but the original owner could claim the merchandise. The dealer who bought stolen antiques had no legal recourse. It was a prickly situation, but if the probable thief had gone to Alex with the van, he could have demanded proof of ownership and had the police close by in case none was supplied.

She still didn't have her own key to the gallery, but Alex was there waiting for her.

"Hard day?" he asked sympathetically.

"Rough in spots." She told him about the man trying to sell the lamp.

"I couldn't have handled it better myself," he said.

His approval was like a balm, and she forgot about being tired.

"I had Blanche type out a one-year employment contract. You can take a copy home and study it before you sign." He handed her a white business-size envelope, and, somehow managing to contain her curiosity about her salary, she slipped it into her purse unread.

"Before we quit for the day, I'll explain the security system to you," he said, "and here're your keys. The small one is for the file. Blanche has the third key, and only the three of us have access to clients' records."

Giving her the keys was a sign of trust, and she accepted them with a deep sense of responsibility. The security system wasn't complicated, but it seemed highly effective. Anyone entering the building when it was locked for the night, whether they used a key or not, had two minutes to call the security firm and give a code number. If this wasn't done, armed policemen would immediately be dispatched to cover both exits. The last thing Alex did before leaving was to call the number and check out. Her father would enjoy hearing about this system. Unlike most of his trusting friends and neighbors, he was a great believer in burglar protection. Anyone attempting to steal merchandise consigned to one of his sales and stored in the auction barn would come face to face with a pair of very well-trained Dobermans. They were people-loving watchdogs, but it was unlikely anyone would linger in their presence long enough to learn that.

"Now dinner?" Alex asked.

"Meals are included in the job?" She wanted to go with him so badly, she had to cover by joking.

"They're not in the contract, but you'd be making a lonely bachelor happy."

"A lonely bachelor? That sounds like someone's old uncle home with a stinky pipe and shabby slippers."

"If you can see through my line in one day, I'm in big trouble. But I do hate eating alone."

Remembering Mrs. Webster, she doubted if solitary dining was forced on him often.

"I shouldn't look a gift horse in the mouth."

Laughing, he said, "I didn't think anyone still said that."

"Probably not, but Dad's auction spiel has rubbed off on me. It's a little cornball sometimes, but the bidders seem to love it."

"Good auctioneers are always entertainers. Stir up competition and keep people in suspense."

"Dad's formula exactly."

"There's a little place I know with great steaks and chicken . . ."

In the candle-lit atmosphere of the restaurant she thoroughly enjoyed telling him about her day. He laughed over the old lady with the doll, agreeing that she probably knew as much about antiques as they did.

"Was Myra miffed because I wasn't there?" He tried to slip the question in casually, but Kate was sure she detected an edge of concern in his voice.

"Myra?" It wasn't her style to play dumb, but the mention of Chairperson Webster made her forget the delicious orange sauce on the chicken.

"Webster. She was heading up the show. Didn't you meet her?"

"Oh, yes." She ate another bite, pretending to search her memory. "I think she said something about Saturday."

"Must mean her party a week from tomorrow. She always has a big bash after the show to thank her committee. I have it on my calendar. You might as well come with me."

"I may have other plans," she said stiffly.

"Oh? You're getting acquainted fast." He didn't sound particularly pleased.

So far she'd exchanged nods with one neighbor, a rather vacant-faced woman who walked a gray poodle, and said good morning to the young couple who lived across the hall. They looked about sixteen and eighteen and giggled a lot.

"I like to settle in fast."

"I know I'm a slave driver sometimes, but this is an important party for you to attend. Several very good clients will be there."

"Is Mrs. Webster one?"

"Yes. Since her divorce settlement she's been investing heavily in silver. I sold her a pair of Georgian sauceboats last fall."

"You did warn me this isn't a nine-to-five business."

"You'll go, then?"

"All right." But it wasn't likely she'd ever sell anything to Myra Webster.

A steady rain was falling when they left the restaurant; the street looked shiny under the reflection of the lights. The heavy moist air trapped odors, giving the city a metallic, slightly fishy smell. Drops clung to the waterproof surface of her coat but soaked into Alex's suit jacket, darkening the light buff shoulders. He hadn't bothered to take his car—he said parking was more trouble than hailing a cab—but he swore softly when the third occupied taxi drove past him splashing dirty water on his pants.

"My apartment is only three blocks from here," he said. "Would you mind making a dash for it, and I can drive you home?"

"Maybe I can get a bus?" she offered, just to be polite.

"No, I'll drive you."

He took her hand and they did dash, trying to leap over puddles but more often splashing down in the middle, sprinting then walking, laughing when he danced on one foot, his other soaked by a deep stream forming in the gutter. By the time they reached the awning over the entrance to his building, her shoes had become squishy and her hose soaked to the knees. A doorman extended an umbrella as they approached, and he greeted Alex as Mr. Gilbert. Kate was a little embarrassed by the wet tracks they left on the dark polished floor of the vestibule, and the sight of a security guard at a desk in front of a TV monitor reminded her that she was indeed stepping into a different world. In Butterfield only the sheriff's deputies wore uniforms, and they were kept busy clocking teenage speeders and maintaining order on Saturday nights.

Alex's apartment didn't disappoint her. A sofa and chairs upholstered in brown tweed were masculine, modern, comfortable, and had massive armrests. The pale beige carpeting tied in these pieces with an eclectic assortment of antiques, the finest being a secretary with claw-and-ball feet and a mellow brown patina. But it wasn't the furniture that dominated; across the room huge windows overlooked the city, and one side wall was completely covered by a spacious glass-fronted display cabinet housing Alex's precious stringed instruments.

Following his lead, she slipped off her shoes in the small entryway, leaving them to ooze on a utilitarian throw rug. She trailed after him into the room, hoping her wet panty hose wouldn't make marks on the light carpeting.

"You're almost as wet as I am," he said, looking at her feet. "Why don't you use the bath off the guest room to dry off while I change?"

This room was done in red and dark honey tan, the bedspread a crimson expanse that picked up the color of the

44

Mercedes-Benz in a striking pre–World War I poster. The woman in the foreground wore a great honey-toned plumed hat that almost hid her profile, and several other women in ankle-length dresses were entering the chauffeur-driven car. The sophisticated poster dominated the decor and almost made her forget her cold, wet feet.

She peeled off her panty hose and squeezed out the water, then wadded them into a tight ball that she hoped would not dampen anything important in her purse. Washing her feet and legs with a thick, steamy washcloth gave her a delicious sensation, but now she felt awkward as she returned to the living room bare-legged like a farm girl. Her winter-pale legs looked silly against the edge of her camel-colored skirt.

Alex had changed into jeans and a soft white pullover that made his hair look even blacker. She found him in the kitchen absorbed in concocting drinks at a counter that looked like an oversize butcher's block. He didn't hear her approach on bare feet, which gave her a chance to watch him unobserved for a few minutes. There was a sureness about his movements that made him seem at ease no matter what he was doing; his was a natural grace, which only a few Thoroughbred racehorses and especially blessed humans seemed to have. Her fingers ached to trace the outline of his shoulders, to slip around his slim waist so she could press her cheek against the downy wool of his sweater. Yet, no matter how much she wanted to be in his arms, he made her feel unaccountably shy. It seemed incredible that he should want to spend time with her. She was a barn cat and he was a purebred Siamese.

He turned and smiled. "Are your feet cold? I can get you some socks."

"No, they're fine."

"This hot rum toddy will warm you up. Nothing like it after running in the spring rain. Go sit in the living room, and I'll bring it in a minute."

Curling up in one of the oversize chairs, tucking her feet

under the folds of her skirt, she admired the light-speckled view beyond the water-streaked surface of the big windows. The room could be called a music room. A poster for an Italian opera set the mood; it hung in solitary splendor over the couch, its yellow and brown tones perfect for the surroundings.

"Are you your own decorator?" she asked when he returned to hand her a warm white mug and a thick paper napkin.

"I'm good at telling people what I want—not at doing it myself."

"Umm." She tested the rim of the cup and decided not to risk scalding her tongue. "That's the important part."

"I wonder. Sometimes I'd much rather create something as beautiful as the things I sell, but my lone talent is plucking out a few tunes on a mandolin."

"Hardly a small talent!" She was dying to ask if he'd made up the song "Oh, Katie, My Love," but didn't dare. "Do you play often?"

He didn't take this as a hint to play, much to her regret. Maybe it was better that he didn't. She was much more comfortable thinking of him as her employer than as a spellbinding ballad singer. They talked easily about an upcoming auction, an estate he had appraised in Southport, a new exhibit scheduled at the Met. Slowly sipping her toddy, she felt her eyelids grow heavy.

"Poor kid," he said, walking over to relieve her of the nearly empty mug. "I can't expect you to put in eighteen hours every day."

"This isn't work." She smiled dreamily and wiggled her toes under her skirt to restore their circulation.

Setting both mugs on a table beside the chair, he bent over, touching her chin, finding her lips, and pressing his mouth against them. It was a long, still, incredibly exciting caress, not a kiss but more than a kiss. Warm currents

46

flowed through her, and when he straightened himself up, she unthinkingly whispered, "I like that."

"I hope so."

He pulled her up from the chair and into his arms and continued what he had started, slowly moving his lips against hers like a blind man memorizing new terrain. Opening his mouth, he covered hers, tasting and teasing, sucking delight from the softness. Whatever other talents he possessed, he was a master at kissing, bringing more to the questing contact of their mouths than most men brought to bed. He made her eager to explore the slippery recesses of his mouth with her tongue, inviting her to imitate what he was doing with such devastating effectiveness.

Turning her head to catch her breath, she impulsively whispered, "No one should kiss like that."

"Like what?" He looked down at her, pleasure softening his features.

"Like you do."

Not a brilliant answer but it seemed to satisfy him.

There was nothing slow or tentative about his next kiss, jolting her as it did to the tips of her bare toes which she dug into the thick pile of the carpet to keep her balance. His hands moved from the tops of her shoulders down the silk-covered lengths of her arms, capturing her fingers and bringing them to the front of his sweater.

"Are you warm now?" His arms circled her waist as he drew her closer, showing her she'd only received lesson one in his kissing curriculum.

"I'd like to do more than kiss you," he whispered softly, transferring his attention to an especially sensitive spot behind her ear.

How could she think straight with Alex's hands edging up her sides, almost accidentally brushing her breasts? For goodness' sake! She'd gone steady with Randy for two years before his frustration and her curiosity brought them together in the back of his father's van. How could she go to work in the morning if Alex thought she was a pushover, tumbling into bed with him the second day she'd known him?

"I think—" she started to say, but he didn't give her a chance to come up with the clever, witty rejection calculated to keep them on good terms.

"You think you'd better go home and read your contract?"

"I couldn't put it better myself," she said uncomfortably.

"But you're not angry?" He held her face between his hands, his expression showing disappointment but not blame.

"Oh, no."

"And one more little kiss can't hurt?"

"I don't see how it could."

Her lips parted, welcoming him with more gusto than any man would expect from a woman who had just said no.

"You taste delicious," he murmured.

"It's your toddy."

"If I kiss you again, you won't go home tonight."

"Oh, you think so!"

His self-confidence was just a little too much! She flounced away, finding her still-damp shoes and, with a shudder, thrusting warm toes against the cold, soggy lining. As he stood watching her with a bemused stare, she admitted the truth to herself: One more kiss would be enough to keep her there.

"I'll get my car keys," he said.

"Oh, no! I mean, no, thank you, that won't be necessary. I'll take a cab home."

"I'd like to drive you."

"But there's no parking in my neighborhood. I'd just jump out of the car and run upstairs. I can take a taxi for that."

"I might get lucky. And find a parking space."

"No, I'm sure you wouldn't. Not tonight."

"Maybe you're right." He smiled, and she wanted to kiss him but knew that would be foolhardy. How often could a mouse expect to get its tail free of the lion's paw?

"Well, thank you for the dinner." She was struggling into her coat after finding it herself in the entryway closet.

"At least let me walk you to the cab."

"Your doorman will get one for me, won't he?"

"Yes, but I'm not dangerous in elevators."

He was teasing, and she wasn't sure whether to be angry or relieved.

"I certainly hope not."

He didn't touch her in the elevator, and down on the sidewalk he stood several feet away, stepping forward only after the doorman had opened a taxi door for her. Alex took her hand as she turned to get into the vehicle, bringing it to his lips and softly kissing it.

"That was a safe kiss," he said.

As the cab pulled away from the curb, she twisted her hands together, unwilling to admit she was actually trembling. There was no such thing as a safe kiss from Alex Gilbert.

CHAPTER THREE

Honey dripped with maddening slowness from the spout of a plastic container shaped like a bear, dotting the slice of whole wheat toast with sticky little droplets. The steaming water in the brown china teapot with yellow enameled flowers was seeping through the tea bag, releasing the scent of fresh-picked mint. Kate gave the honey bear an impatient squeeze and soaked half of the toast with golden syrup; she hurriedly pumped the tea bag up and down in the water, finally pulling it out and leaving a trail of drops all the way to the sink. She was running late, and breakfast hardly seemed worth the bother. What she did have to do before going to work was sign her contract. Why had she neglected it all weekend?

Biting off a corner of toast, she got her fingers gooey and had to wash them before taking the typed contract from her purse. It was a simple document with a copy for her records and one to be returned. The terms were very agreeable; the one-year salary, which was more than what she'd made at the museum, would more than cover the higher cost of living in the city. Fringe benefits included medical and other insurance plans. She signed one copy and put it back in her purse to return to the gallery.

This tangible proof that her ability was recognized should have given her Monday morning a great start. Instead she dressed reluctantly and then walked to the bus stop with growing doubts. Certainly she could do the work and do it well, but what about her feelings for Alex? Could she walk into the gallery and pretend his kisses hadn't touched her? Could she look at him without wanting to feel his arms around her?

After worrying all weekend and not hearing from him, she almost welcomed the news that he was in Connecticut and would be working there for several days, if not all week. He would be staying in his apartment in the village of Candlebrook while several important dealers came to look at a new shipment from the Netherlands.

Kate found herself swamped with work for the special display of late-nineteenth-century American art glass planned for the next week. Purchasing this distinguished collection had been a coup for Alex. She wished he could be there to give her some guidelines, but both Blanche and Nancy were knowledgeable and helpful, convincing her they had, in fact, been hired for their competence, not the dignity of their age. Blanche had been working for Alex since the opening of his gallery; her husband had a heart condition that had forced him to take an early retirement. Having been a full-time wife and mother for twenty years, the secretary had reentered the working world with doubts about her own capabilities, but working for Alex had restored her confidence and encouraged her to take a few night courses to upgrade her skills. Nancy Hume had worked in the gallery before Alex bought out the former owner, and her tremendous grasp of the retail side of the business had been appreciated by the new owner. Kate was delighted to be part of a smooth-working team that functioned without rivalries in their employer's absence.

Alex phoned frequently but didn't return, sometimes speaking to Kate himself but more often depending on Blanche to relay his messages. When he rang her apartment Thursday evening, it wasn't a business call.

"How's your week going?" he asked, his voice more mellow now that he wasn't giving orders or checking on the progress of the art-glass display.

"Fine, I'm in love with the pink bride's basket," she said, mentioning an especially pretty Victorian glass piece in delicate rose and pink, shading to white, with tiny enameled flowers. Antiques seemed the only safe topic with Alex.

"I'm sorry I couldn't be there this week. The warehouse here is overstocked and needed my attention."

"Nancy and Blanche have really helped me. The display will be ready on time."

"I'm not worried about it. Your curator in Ohio said you were an artist in working up displays."

This surprised her. Horace's only reaction to her exhibits at the museum had been an occasional grunt.

"Your contract is satisfactory?" Alex asked.

"I signed it, yes."

"I know you signed it. That's not what I asked."

"Very satisfactory, thank you."

"My other New York employees receive full pay during the month of August when the gallery is closed. You will next year."

"I wouldn't expect a month's paid vacation after working such a short time. Half pay is very generous. Thank you." She tried for sincerity but sounded stiff.

Even though the breeze coming through the partially open window was cold enough to make her shiver, a thin film of moisture formed over her upper lip. The walls of the apartment, painted the color of Swiss cheese in a misguided attempt to make the room appear larger, seemed to close in on her, and she nibbled on her lower lip, wondering how to walk the tightrope between being Alex's employee and—and what? Was her contract just a little too generous? No, darn it! She was good in her field and had had years of study and on-the-job training. She deserved a chance at a challenging job and couldn't let personal feelings undermine her confidence.

"I wanted to remind you about Saturday night," he said. "The party. You're still planning on going?"

"Yes." She was counting the hours until then, with a curious mixture of dread, excitement, and sheer longing to be with him again.

"I'm staying here until Saturday morning. How does seven sound? We'll have dinner first."

"Fine."

There was a long pause. Was he expecting her to say more? She couldn't imagine him at a loss for words.

"Anything goes at Myra's parties. Wear whatever you like," he said.

"What will you wear?"

"A suit, I guess." He didn't seem to have given it any thought.

Was he worried because her blue dress had been too schoolgirlish for the rug dealer's affair?

"Well, I'll see you at seven, then," she said.

"Yes, at seven."

She wanted to keep talking, but not about his business or the party or antiques or contracts.

"Blanche and Nancy have been kind and very helpful."

"Good, I want you to feel at home. Well, I'll see you Saturday."

"At seven."

"At seven," he repeated.

She wanted to scream! Was this a date or business appointment they were talking about?

"Good night, then," she said softly.

"Good night, Kate."

There, they had said it, but still neither one broke off the connection.

"I really am sorry—being gone all week with you new to the job."

Did he have to mention the job again? But, of course, the gallery was more than just a business to him.

"Things are going very well. Nancy sold the tea chest. Did she tell you?"

"No. That's good news."

She couldn't stand it anymore. "Good-bye, Alex."

"Until Saturday." He hung up.

Replacing the receiver, she desperately wanted to get away from the tiny apartment with its uninviting hide-a-bed, but where could a single woman who knew no one go on a Thursday night? Walking the streets at night made her nervous, and she had never gone to a movie by herself. Instead she tried to wear herself out finishing the unpacking. The decorative things Linda had left behind she now stored in boxes, pushing them to the back of the deep closet, glad to stow away a bunch of little green frames holding dried weeds and flowers, probably one of her friend's do-it-yourself projects. She covered the discolored spots on the wall with a large unsigned oil painting of a farm at sunset, the buildings and silo black against an orange and yellow sky. In its plain pine frame the painting didn't do a thing for the utilitarian green carpeting or the gray and green striped upholstery of the furniture, and she wasn't sure why she'd bothered to bring it, let alone hang it. She hadn't lived at home on a full-time basis since leaving for college; was it a belated case of homesickness that prompted her to hang an uninspired amateur painting she'd impulsively hauled all the way to New York?

Saturday came, but it didn't bring unmixed joy at the prospect of going to the party with Alex. She would have loved to sweep up her hair and pretend to be sophisticated, but a small hand mirror caught the reflection, in the bathroom mirror, of the still-noticeable pink scar at the back of her neck. Who would believe that a little hair-dryer burn would take so long to fade? Before moving to New York, she'd been proud of her carefully planned wardrobe with its mix of solid basic pieces and imaginative accessories, many of them antiques: gorgeous chain-mesh evening bags, filmy silk scarves, outrageous Art Deco jewelry, even a fur muff that was highly impractical but deliciously warm. Now all her cute touches seemed provincial and her clothing treasures outdated. Before meeting Alex she would have worn her lovely white Victorian dress with a wide ruffle at the hem, which stopped just above her ankles, and pale ivory embroidery on the big collar and cuffs. Here in the big city she just didn't have enough nerve.

When he came for her, she was wearing her all-purpose black dress which she tried not to compare unfavorably with the one Nancy had worn to work on Tuesday. Her shoes with matching purse were of snakeskin in a gray and white variegated pattern—a steal at an estate sale; though miraculously modern-looking with narrow straps across the toes, the shoes were unfortunately half a size too small. She decided to grin and bear it. It was raining again. Was there some natural law that a deluge would fall on this city every weekend?

To save time, she locked her apartment and met Alex in the downstairs entryway, running out to the double-parked cab with him and getting her hair wet because her building lacked an awning.

"It's good to see you," he said. He opened the door for her, then walked around to the driver's side before she could slide over to make room for him. This time he wore a raincoat, British in cut and of a pale fawn fabric that the rain did not penetrate.

"I was going to make room for you on this side," she said as he got in.

"Just playing gentleman," he said, smiling, then gave the driver directions.

Dinner was not an unqualified success. Alex sent his steak back because it was too rare, and hers came with a charcoal coat of its own. Refusing his offer to return it, too, she ate most of it rather than make a fuss. This seemed to annoy him, so she followed his lead and ordered a grasshopper

55

after dinner, even though she didn't want a drink. Besides detesting gourmet food, Alex had a sweet tooth. She wondered how he stayed so slender and fit, but didn't want to ask. She had to work at keeping her weight down with a daily diet of healthy breakfasts and skimpy lunches. Their conversation didn't diverge from antiques until they'd left the restaurant.

"I missed you," he said, speaking softly as he tried to hail a cab in the rainy street.

She wasn't even sure she'd heard him right.

Myra Webster's apartment wasn't spacious by Nebraska standards, but she seemed to have used the palace at Versailles as her model in decorating it. No bit of wall space was unadorned; the moldings were extremely ornate, and huge paintings occupied gesso frames six inches thick. The furniture was old and fine but so fragile it didn't invite occupancy. In fact, no one was sitting, and standing room was at a premium. A man dressed like a footman in a comic opera took their coats, and a maid in a black uniform and a starched cap and apron held a silver tray of champagne goblets under their noses before they had moved three steps. Mixing the bubbly wine with the unwanted grasshopper would be enough to start a game of leapfrog in her stomach, but she took a glass anyway to occupy her hands.

To his credit, Alex tried to make the party enjoyable for her. He introduced her to a number of people, including a man who collected paperweights and was more than willing to talk about them—endlessly. Myra showed how cagey she could be; the older woman, chic in a low-cut white sequined dress that ended three inches above her striking legs, latched onto Alex while the paperweight collector was showing Kate a picture of his latest acquisition which was featured in an antiques magazine he found artfully displayed on a coffee table, one of several with inlaid tops. He was astonished that she didn't know all about the paperweight collection at the Art Institute in Chicago, but tried to make up for this grave

56

omission in her education by describing in detail most of the major examples. Kate listened with a good show of patience; if she ducked away from his lecture, she would probably be left standing alone. Alex was nowhere in sight.

A fidgety little wife reclaimed the paperweight collector, saying he was needed as a fourth for bridge in the game room. Kate deposited her warm but untouched goblet of champagne on a passing tray and wandered into the densely packed dining area. A young man in shiny blue slacks and a white satin shirt stood at the buffet table alternately popping tidbits into his mouth and loading a gold-rimmed Haviland plate with everything in sight.

"Umm, try this," he said, holding a morsel of cake under her nose, giving her no choice but to open her mouth. "Pineapple macadamia. It's almost worth being on Myra's committee to get in on these goodies."

"Very tasty," Kate said politely, regretting that her curiosity about exotic foods was dulled by Alex's disappearance.

"Take a plate," the man urged, thrusting one into her hand. "Don't let me be the only one here stuffing my face at a dollar a bite."

She laughed.

"Try some smoked salmon. Luscious! Pâté with truffles. You won't get that at the Automat. Ah, caviar. Do you know, they hand sort the eggs while the ship's still at sea?"

He fixed a cracker for her, and she nibbled at it.

"Here you are." Alex came up behind her just as her fellow gourmet fixed another cracker and was about to aim it at her mouth. Stiffening in irritation at Alex's tone, she wanted to point out that he'd wandered off, not she.

"Are you ready to leave?" she asked.

"I'm willing, but Myra wants me to meet a couple who're moving to Florida to retire. They have a few good pieces I may want to buy."

"How long do these parties last?"

"Until the last guests go, but we won't be here then, I promise."

He put his arm around her waist, giving her cause to hope that he wouldn't disappear again.

"The Jordans are here, darling," Myra said, descending on Alex just when he had led Kate to an unoccupied corner. "They're dying to meet you."

Kate tried to slip away, but Alex took a no-nonsense hold on her arm and propelled her toward an older couple, whom Myra addressed as John and Mary. The Jordans, who were both tall and round-shouldered, looked like brother and sister and had just celebrated their forty-second wedding anniversary. Kate wondered if they had looked so much alike when they were young and first falling in love. Certainly Alex couldn't pass as her brother, not with his black hair and dark brown eyes. He made her feel pale and washed out; her eyes were not even true blue but a changeable color that sometimes suggested gray.

"My assistant, Kate Bevan," Alex was saying.

She shook hands, then her mind wandered from the conversation. Was Alex's whole life one long business appointment? Did he do anything just for pleasure? Was there anything he enjoyed more than dealing in antiques? He seemed to be part of a network of people, all giving favors and seeking returns. Who were Myra's real friends at this party? Was there anyone there who didn't owe her or wasn't being repaid by her? Life in the fast lane wasn't all that glamorous if it meant an endless series of joyless gatherings and shallow social events.

Alex kept her by his side as he moved from group to group, but the conversational ball never seemed to be in her court. She felt like a professional listener until at last he caught her trying to hide a yawn.

"Would you like to go?" he whispered.

"Only if you're ready."

His hand slipped lower from its resting place on her waist. "I'm more than ready."

Outside, the rain had stopped, and Alex was able to snare a cab.

"Where would you like to go? Any place that doesn't serve raw fish is fine with me," he teased.

"It's pretty late."

"Not too late for a drink?"

He dropped his arm across the back of her shoulders, spreading his legs so one knee crowded against hers. In the close confines of the cab his after-shave suggested sailing ships carrying spices from the Orient, a sweet erotic tang faint enough to make her want to snuggle closer. When he casually moved his arm to rest his palm on her thigh, she felt the intimacy of his touch through layers of clothing.

"I'd really rather go home," she insisted, faking a yawn.

Was she being cowardly or self-protective? Sleepiness had nothing to do with her doubts about prolonging the evening, but she was willing to have Alex believe it did.

"Poor kid, I really threw you into the deep end this week. No wonder you're tired."

He gave the driver her address, then cradled her head on his shoulder. She'd never felt less drowsy in her life.

Quickly pulling some bills from his money clip, he thrust them into the driver's hand and followed Kate up the steps to the front door of her building.

"You've lost your taxi," she said.

"There's always another one."

"I thought cabs disappear when it starts to rain."

"Haven't you noticed? It stopped raining."

With his arm around her, pressing her hip against his side, she wouldn't notice a hurricane.

"So it has." She hated her nervous giggle. "Thank you for the evening."

The clasp on the snakeskin bag was being temperamental;

she retrieved her keys but couldn't get it to stay shut. He pretended not to notice, taking her key ring from her.

"I hate to make you trudge up three flights," she said without much conviction.

"I won't need oxygen at the top. I work out three times a week at a health club."

That explained his trim body; it didn't tell her what would happen if he followed her into her apartment.

"It's only a studio apartment, but I guess I was lucky to sublet it."

"Don't apologize," he said a little gruffly. "I'm not a snob."

"I wasn't intimating that you were!"

She didn't need to explain to him that the same key fit the regular lock and the bolt lock.

"It's cold in here," he said, shutting the door behind them.

"I left a window open. It always seems so stuffy in here." She walked over and closed it, wishing she'd taken down the threadbare lace curtains. The window would look better bare than with the yellowing old things that came with the apartment.

"Nebraska?" he asked, walking over to look at her painting.

"It's pretty bad, I know," she said, afraid that he would begin to doubt her taste.

"So bad it's almost good? I like it." His smile told her that he liked her. "Do you mind if I take off my coat?"

"I'm sorry. Let me hang it up."

"Don't bother."

He draped it over the back of a comfortable platform rocker she had brought with her. She'd been reluctant to abandon it, having restored its golden oak finish herself reupholstering it in dark brown crushed velvet.

"And don't apologize," he added. "I invited myself. I hope you don't mind."

"No, I don't." She took his coat and hung it up anyway, needing to do something besides stare at him.

His eyes searched her face, but she found it impossible to meet his gaze.

"My beverage selection isn't great. Orange juice or tea?"

"I didn't come here to drink, and you're apologizing again." She wasn't imagining the threat in his voice as he moved closer and said, "Don't do that."

It took some effort to bite back the word "Sorry."

"Aren't you going to take your coat off?" he asked.

More than ever she felt like the little mouse with its tail caught. How could he make her feel like his professional equal when they talked business, then reduce her to a shy, gawky girl by looking at her the way he was doing now? With deliberate slowness she slipped out of her coat and hung it in the single roomy closet, wishing for a panicky instant that she could disappear into the dark depths where Linda's junk was stored.

"Maybe a glass of ice water?" she suggested.

"Fine."

He followed her to the kitchen alcove, watching intently while she popped cubes out of the plastic ice tray and filled two glasses to the brim, then handed him one and sipped from the other. He quickly drained the glass and took hers from her.

"I've spent one hellishly long week regretting that I didn't kiss you one more time."

"Alex—" His mouth covered hers before she could decide whether to protest.

Memory hadn't deceived her; this kiss was everything she'd remembered his first ones to be: gentle and penetrating. His mouth moved against hers forcefully, delightfully possessing her.

Touching his face with first one hand and then both, she felt the hard cheekbones and the slight crookedness of his nose that robbed his face of conventional male beauty.

61

"It's been broken," he said, reading her mind as he locked her in his arms, first nibbling at her lips, then kissing them with great gusto.

"How?" She tried to slow her breathing, but the hands caressing her shoulders and neck made her wildly excited.

"My ill-fated hockey career. I gave it up when I started college."

"Is there anything you haven't done?"

She immediately knew this question was poorly phrased.

"With you there is." He slid his hands down her back, spreading his fingers over her somewhat bouncy bottom, making her acutely conscious of every move he made. "But I hope to remedy that."

She tried to back away and only succeeded in getting squeezed against the cupboard separating the sink and stove.

"I think we should talk," she managed to say.

He slowly slid the zipper down her back, nuzzling her neck, then he looked into her face.

"It seems a terrible waste of time."

She hated the trace of a whimper in her voice, but he was slowly reducing her to a quivering mass of nerves.

"Come here." He led her to the couch, pulling her down beside him. "I think I know what you're going to say."

"You do?" She didn't know herself.

"We've just met, I'm your employer, and I'm taking advantage of you. You're not ready for this, you need more time, and won't I please slow down?"

"Is that what women usually say to you?" His arm was heavy against her shoulders, but it gave her an unwanted feeling of security.

"There aren't any other women in my life right now."

"Not Myra Webster?"

"Lord no!" He laughed. "I'm not interested in being anyone's fourth husband."

Or anyone's first husband, she thought dejectedly.

"Look at me." He touched her cheek with the back of his

fingers, then slid them down to the scoop neckline of her dress, reaching under the layers of fabric to caress the swell of her breast.

His fingers were cool, but not unpleasantly so, as he stroked the fleshy mound. Not until she met his eyes and he read the willingness there did he slide a single finger over her nipple, teasing it to excited hardness.

"It will be so good for both of us," he said softly. "You're the freshest, loveliest thing I've seen in years."

"But I'm not a thing." She felt like unformed clay being molded under the exploring tips of his fingers.

"Woman." He made the word sound like a sorcerer's spell.

Why couldn't she do as her heart dictated, and show that she wanted him as much as he wanted her? Certainly she was old enough; one great-aunt in Nebraska was predicting the dire fate of spinsterhood for her.

"Alex—"

His kiss was too marvelous to resist, but when he deftly slid the dress from her shoulders, she felt oddly vulnerable. He removed her bra just as easily, fingering the black lacy cups for a moment before tossing it aside and leaning over, bending to kiss her naked breasts. His tongue flicked in and out, and he used his lips with a skill that left her gasping for breath. She was being aroused by an expert—he stimulated her with as much finesse as he had applied to playing the mandolin. It was heady and exciting, a sensual excursion into almost unbearable pleasures. When his hand slid between her thighs, parting and then stroking them, she wanted nothing more than to put herself totally in his hands.

He felt her shudder and mistook it for passion, standing to free them both of their clothing. His jacket was on the floor, and his shirt unbuttoned, before he realized she was dressing, not undressing.

"I can't, Alex. I'm really sorry."

All she could see was the taut circle of his navel and a

sprinkling of hairs that disappeared under his belt line. Afraid that her face would contradict her words, she did not look at him.

"You're apologizing again."

She had expected anger, not the understanding softness of his voice.

"I shouldn't have let it go this far," she whispered hoarsely.

He stood closer and cupped her chin, forcing her to look at him.

"I'm the one who should apologize, but I'm not going to." His little half smile was filled with self-mockery. "I always bid on what I want."

"But you don't always win?" If she answered his smile, she would make a fool of herself by crying.

"No, but there's always another day."

"Another sale?"

"Yes."

"But I'm not merchandise, Alex."

"I never suggested you were." He kissed the tips of her fingers one by one, nearly undoing all her resolve.

"I don't know how I can show up for work on Monday," she said miserably.

He stood and stared at her for a long moment.

"There's no way you can not show up. We have a contract, Kate."

"I'm willing to tear it up."

"I'm not."

"Even—even—" She didn't know how to ask.

"There's nothing in the contract that says you have to sleep with me," he said sarcastically enough to bring a deep flush to her face.

"How can you—"

"I want you because you're beautiful and intriguing. I hired you because you're qualified. One has nothing to do with the other."

She wanted to believe him, but her breasts still felt damp from his tongue and her thighs were quivering, even though she tightened them together with all her strength.

"I just don't think it will work." She couldn't work with him pretending she didn't want him, but it would be even worse to have a casual affair and then to be dropped for a younger version of Myra Webster, someone who belonged in his world.

"Damn!" He turned away and pounded a fist into his palm. "It will work."

"You stepped on your jacket."

They laughed because they needed to laugh, not because a footprint on the finely woven charcoal cloth was funny.

"Working with you isn't going to be dull," he said with a good-humored smile.

"You really think this won't matter?"

"Of course it matters! I'm not going to stop trying, Katie. Not even if you refuse to work for me. I'll follow you to Nebraska if necessary."

"You wouldn't really do that?"

"Are you going to find out the hard way?"

She wanted to toss his challenge back at him, but not if it meant sacrificing a job she desperately wanted. She hadn't even been to a New York City auction yet!

"No, I really want to work for you."

"Good." He slowly bent over and retrieved his jacket. "Kate, are you a virgin?"

A flood of boiling blood rushed to her head, and she wanted the floor to drop out from under her.

"The boys in Nebraska don't ask?" His words were mocking, but there was an undertone of affection in his voice.

"No one with manners does!" Her outburst made her feel even more foolish.

"Maybe I do owe you an apology for asking." His grin was sheepish now.

"You just can't believe your fatal charm didn't work."

"No, I can't believe a woman as warm and desirable as you wants to turn off her feelings."

"Maybe I don't feel that way about you!"

"No?"

She felt a strong urge to slap the aggravating smile off his face.

"I'd appreciate it if you'd go."

"I will. May I have my coat?"

She had found her own coat at his apartment. Did that mean her manners were lacking too, or was he trying to extract a bit of personal service as his revenge?

"It's in the closet."

"Thank you." He found it and put it on in silence. "I have some press people coming Monday morning. Maybe we'll get some publicity for the art glass. Can you come a little early, say, seven thirty, so we can go over things?"

"Yes, I'll be there."

"I'm going to a friend's on Long Island tomorrow."

"You don't need to tell me."

"No, but I want you to know I'll be thinking about you even if I don't call."

"It would be better if you didn't."

"Think or call?"

"Both."

"And you won't give me a thought all day tomorrow?"

"My job is always on my mind."

"It is?" He buried his hand in her hair and kissed her almost savagely, ignoring her ineffective struggles.

"You can't wipe kisses out of your memory that way," he said, watching her run the back of her hand over the tender skin around her mouth.

"I *am* going to quit!"

"I'm not," he said, his voice low but emphatic. "But you're safe at work, Katie. I promise to treat you exactly as I do any other employee when we're at the gallery or out on business together. Is that fair?"

"Yes," she agreed, regretting her impulsive threat to quit. "If you mean it."

"I told you, I can separate business from pleasure. You can trust me at the gallery, but in return you have to guarantee to live up to your contract."

"You won't have any reason to complain about my work," she said dryly.

"And you won't have to worry about your employer taking advantage of you—on the job."

"That's the only place I'll be seeing you."

This time his smile was broad, revealing square white teeth that were even except for one on top that was slightly crooked. Funny how his little flaws only made him more appealing.

She was just turning the bolt lock after his departure when a sharp rap sounded on the door. It had to be Alex; he hadn't had time to move away. After fumbling with the lock, she inched the door open.

"I forgot to tell you," he said teasingly, "I love the way your freckles stand out when you blush."

The slam of the door echoed all the way to the bottom landing.

CHAPTER FOUR

Kate fastened a little metal tag on the lapel of her white lightweight blazer and joined the flow of patrons who had made their donation to the Metropolitan Museum of Art. Glancing through the guidebook as she walked, she felt pulled in a dozen different directions, wanting to see all three million objects in the vast collection spanning five thousand years of human history, but knowing it would take days just to view those currently on public display. The sheer size of the building was exciting, making her feel like an explorer about to discover fabulous treasures, in spite of the Saturday crowd. She wasn't going to spoil this day by thinking about Alex.

He'd kept his word, maintaining a businesslike attitude throughout the working day, only rarely betraying his interest by looking in her direction a moment longer than necessary. Some men undressed women with their eyes; he went further, seemingly trying to see inside her mind, her heart, her soul. Brief as these flashes of attention were, they were disconcerting, making her appreciate the busy hours that filled her days, whether she worked at the gallery or went out on buying excursions. Alex went with her to an important auction featuring Colonial furniture, but for the most part she worked alone, researching and making contacts to lessen his excessive work load. At the end of her second full week she knew he deserved his reputation as a leading dealer.

Deciding to save the American collection for another day because it was so closely related to her work, she plotted a course through the medieval exhibits, hoping to lose herself in daydreams of knights in armor and gallant deeds. Much of her passion for the past was fired by a lively imagination, and trying to picture everyday life in other eras was always exhilarating. Maybe, for a short time, she could forget about Alex and stop regretting her decision not to spend the weekend with him on Long Island. He had taken her rejection philosophically, as he had her five refusals of dinner invitations that week. Was he losing interest, or was he so confident of winning the cat-and-mouse game that her evasiveness was only part of the challenge to him?

She absentmindedly stuffed the map of the museum into her snakeskin purse, forgetting the tricky catch until it popped open, spilling an array of items on the floor. Worried about her apartment keys, she stooped to retrieve them, nearly toppling a man who was walking behind her.

"Oh, I'm sorry!" he said, catching himself by leaning on her shoulders, then quickly backing off. He bent to help her gather the rest of her things.

"It's my fault. Really. I shouldn't have brought a purse that won't stay shut." She took the lipstick and ballpoint he handed her. "Thank you so much."

"I didn't hurt you, stumbling into you like that?"

His hair was a pale silky blond, and he had the kind of fair skin that turned almost crimson when he blushed. As a freckle-faced blusher herself, she felt an instant empathy with him.

"No, not at all." They were causing a traffic obstruction, forcing people to crowd around them on either side. "I guess we're in the way."

"I've felt in the way ever since I got here from Iowa," he said, grinning, his face slowly returning to its natural color.

"Iowa! I'm from Nebraska," she said impulsively. "I'll bet you've never heard of Butterfield."

"No, but I have a cousin just outside of Lincoln. John Carson. Same name as mine, only he's John William and I'm William John. Of course, everyone calls me Bill."

"Bill, thanks for helping me pick up my things."

"Are you here alone?"

"Yes, but . . ."

"I'll tell you, I've been here two weeks, and they've been the longest two weeks of my life. I'd sure like to talk to someone who doesn't think Iowans grow on cornstalks."

She smiled sympathetically. "Will you be here much longer?"

"Another couple of weeks should do it. I'm in the meat business. This is my first trip east for the packinghouse."

"What exhibits do you want to see?"

"I'm just killing time, seeing what there is to see in New York. I thought maybe some of that Egyptian stuff. Unless you'd like to see something else?"

"Egyptian sounds fascinating. Where are you from in Iowa?"

"Originally Adair. Right near where Jesse James pulled the first moving train robbery west of the Mississippi. There's even a marker on the spot."

"Well, that's something to be famous for."

Bill liked medieval armor better than Egyptian tombs, and Kate found herself liking him. He was big and brawny, at least six two with the shoulders and thick neck of a football lineman, which he'd been in high school and junior college. He was interested in seeing everything, although most of it didn't hold his attention long, and he especially wanted to know how Kate liked New Yorkers.

"I guess there are nice people everywhere," she said. "I haven't been here long enough to meet many."

"Everybody's in such a darn big rush. If I have a nine-o'clock appointment, I'd better have my say by nine fifteen or the guy's looking at his watch."

They were walking aimlessly. Bill didn't rush her when

70

she wanted to read a label or examine something closely, but she sensed that he was much more interested in talking about their common midwestern background. Homesickness can hit at any age; she might feel the same way if Alex wasn't constantly on her mind. But for a while, laughing at Bill as he tried and failed to find a suit of armor that might be large enough to fit him, she forgot Alex. Maybe all she needed was a social life—people her own age with whom she could share the many activities possible in this city. She had even started wishing Linda would return early, although doubling up in the tiny apartment with a friend who thought good housekeeping was only a catchy name for a magazine would be an endurance test. The two women at the gallery were friendly, but Blanche was preoccupied with her husband's failing health, and Nancy rode a commuter train for more than an hour each morning and returned to a busy suburban life every evening. When Bill asked her to dinner, she accepted.

The man from Iowa would eat anything, requiring only quantity to make him happy. This didn't make Bill a gourmet, but he was adventurous about dining, suggesting they look through the yellow pages of the phone directory and pick someplace interesting. They settled on a Greek restaurant where he ate everything served to him, with good-natured enjoyment. The avgolemono, a soup made of lemon juice, egg yolks, and chicken stock, was new to her and delicious, as was the salad with feta cheese. The spanakopita, a cheese and spinach appetizer, was excellent, even if the fish eggs and eggplant were mediocre.

"Nice to see a girl who likes food," Bill said.

"I have to starve all week to eat a meal like this," she admitted.

Bill didn't climb the three flights to her apartment, seeming a little relieved when she suggested he keep the taxi instead of seeing her to the door. He joked that he missed his car more than he did his mother, and Kate could sympathize. To people used to owning a car, cabs were an irksome way of getting around town.

Sunday was warm and sunny, the brilliance of the day transforming the city. She walked with Bill for hours in Central Park. They occasionally stopped to toss a Frisbee back and forth, although she spent more time chasing it than catching it. They held hands and exchanged soft companionable kisses along with stories about their childhoods and hometowns.

"I used to think grain silos looked just like castle towers guarding the countryside," she mused.

"When I see them now, all I think about is the price of cattle feed," he admitted, "but it's not a bad life there. Quiet sometimes, but I wouldn't want to raise kids anywhere else."

The expression on his face was unmistakable, but she didn't want to talk about kids. Bill looked a lot like Randy, a big, bearlike man, slow moving but intelligent. She liked him very much, and being with him was a calming and satisfying experience. He was a man who wouldn't change, and a smart woman wouldn't want him to. But this didn't make her ready to ponder a future with him.

For dinner they wandered into an Italian restaurant where Kate was content to nibble from a huge platter of crisp celery, green peppers, olives, carrots, and tomatoes while Bill consumed a cold antipasto down to the last sliver of spicy meat. They then shared an order of rigatoni—fortunately, for Kate found her half of the pasta with highly seasoned sauce more than she could eat.

"I feel like I've eaten my way through the weekend," she said as they walked to the door to her apartment building, hurrying because a taxi was again waiting for Bill at the curb.

"That's not how I feel."

His parting kiss was quick but pleasant.

After writing an overdue letter to her parents and rinsing out her panty hose, she took a long bath in the big old-fashioned tub that was one of the apartment's few assets, then slipped into faded green cotton pajamas. Piling the cushions on a nearby chair, she opened the hide-a-bed and found one of the paperback romances that had become her nighttime companions. A visitor was the last thing she expected, and she responded to the buzzer wondering if Bill had decided to return.

"Kate, it's Alex. May I come up?"

"It's late," she said weakly, trying to discourage herself more than him.

"Still the shank of the evening."

His sardonic tone rankled.

"Alex, I don't think—"

"I'm going to look pretty silly when they find me out cold on your doorstep tomorrow morning still clutching an empty bottle of Bordeaux in a paper bag."

"You don't like French wine."

"I'll pretend it's California."

"Red or white?"

"Which do you prefer?"

"White."

"Then I guessed right."

"You're trying to bribe your way in. Why aren't you on Long Island?"

"Roads go both ways. I can run out for some steamed clams if the wine isn't enough."

"Will you eat some?"

"I don't eat things that look like rubber."

"Are you sober?" He certainly didn't sound like the serious gallery owner.

"Sober enough to go home for my mandolin. Do you want a serenade under your window, or shall I come up?"

"Oh, come up!"

Dashing to the closet, she found her winter robe; the rosy-pink velour garment reached her toes and was about as revealing as a laundry sack. It clashed with her fuzzy red

73

slippers, but Alex didn't give her time to worry about that. A knock sounded as she was zipping up the front.

"How did you get up here so fast?"

"Ran so you didn't have time to change your mind." He thrust the bottle of wine at her and pretended he didn't need to catch his breath.

"Thank you. Shall we leave the door open?"

"Are your neighbors nosy?"

"No, I hardly see them."

"Then we might as well close it." He did, grinning at her in his least trustworthy way.

She'd never seen him dressed so casually. His cotton-knit running suit was a faded red and more than a little baggy in the seat and knees. His once-white jogging shoes were a scuffed gray. Dark ringlets of hair fell over his forehead, and his face was damp, giving him the look of someone who had just run a hard race. He brought an enticingly musky, outdoor smell into the small room.

"Why are you here?" she asked.

"I was out for a run and just happened to be passing by."

"With a bottle of wine?"

"Will a little shaking ruin it?"

"Alex, you shouldn't have come."

"Why not? You like wine, and I like you. You taste my wine, and I'll—"

"Oh, no!"

"Are you wearing pajamas?" He moved into the alcove and searched the cupboards until he found two wineglasses.

"That's not your concern."

"Do you know that wine with a cork will keep working in the bottle, but with a screw cap it's finished. Tastes the same today as next year."

"I thought you weren't interested in wine."

"I asked the man who sold me this bottle why they didn't put caps on all wine. Saves all the bother with corkscrews. Dangerous weapons, corkscrews."

"Are you tipsy?" she asked with renewed suspicion.

"No, I'm a man who's very low pretending to be high."

The wineglass he handed her was so full he had to inch his way toward her to keep from spilling it. He drank his wine in three quick gulps while standing by the kitchen counter.

"Back in the mountains some old-timers believe drinking vinegar will make you live to be a hundred." He plunked the glass down and didn't refill it. "I just bought a few extra days."

"Really, Alex!"

"Really, Alex," he mimicked.

"My brother used to repeat things like that because it made me furious."

"I only want to annoy you; furious sounds too violent."

"You came here just to annoy me?"

"No, I came to make love to you, but on the off chance you say no, I wanted to be sure of some entertainment."

He was an outrageous tease; she didn't want to encourage him, but it was hard to hide her grin. She turned her back on him, walking to the window overlooking the street.

"Haven't I been on good behavior all week?" he asked.

"Do you want a gold star?"

"No, a kiss."

He was directly behind her.

"Alex . . ."

"What did you do all weekend?" He made it sound like a casual, friendly question.

"I went to the Metropolitan Museum of Art."

"And?"

"Ate dinner at a Greek restaurant."

"Alone?"

"No."

"You've met some nice woman who's crazy about foreign food?"

"No."

"Some nice man?"

"You might say that, yes."

"One of my clients?"

"No, I don't like to mix business and pleasure either."

"Where does a nice girl like you meet men in the big city?" He was definitely sounding grumpy.

"At the museum."

He spun her around to face him, keeping hard hands on her shoulders.

"You picked up some guy at the Met?"

"It was not a pickup, and I'm perfectly capable of choosing my own friends."

"This isn't Nebraska, Katie!" He could compress his lips into an almost straight line when he was angry.

"And he didn't try to get me into bed the second time we went out!"

"You've seen him twice?" He didn't let go of her shoulders.

"We walked in the park today and had an Italian dinner."

"I thought I smelled garlic."

"I certainly didn't invite you to get this close!"

"There's nothing inviting about garlic breath."

She tried to duck under his arms, but he wouldn't let her, capturing her waist and holding her against him.

"You could use a shower yourself," she complained, just to get even.

"Where do you keep the towels?" He nuzzled the hollow of her neck and caressed the small of her back.

"You're not using my shower!"

"Some women like their men a little gamy."

"Well, I don't." She squirmed and wriggled but only succeeded in getting trapped in a bear hug.

"Let me kiss you once, then I'll leave if you want me to."

"Promise?"

"Cross my heart." His face was so close she could feel the warmth of his breath.

"You won't like it. I ate lots of garlic: garlic toast, garlic sauce, whole cloves of garlic."

"Don't count on it!"

He sampled her lips, then teased them apart.

"Is the kiss over?" she asked breathlessly.

"It hasn't even started."

She loved it when he ran his fingers through her hair, moving her head as he moved his mouth, bombarding her with the questing tip of his tongue until she captured it against the roof of her mouth.

He lifted her then, carrying her to the open hide-a-bed and lowering her beneath him.

"Don't worry, I'm not going to make love to you tonight," he said softly, gently kissing her eyelids and the tip of her nose.

"Too much garlic?" She turned her head to the side, squirming with pleasure when he kissed her cheek and the lobe of her ear.

"Garlic only keeps vampires away."

"Then it's safe to assume you're not one?"

"Don't assume anything." He hovered over her, his knees on either side of her thighs.

"Are you trying to tell me something?"

She lowered her lids, not wanting to see the look of passion in his eyes. How would it feel to be a man, to have a body that reacted so visibly when stirred by lust? It was a new thought but a bad time to consider it.

"Only that I've never had a partner, and I don't buy shares in anything." He kissed her slowly and thoroughly, making her feel his weight, without crushing her.

"You make it sound like everything has to be your way."

He rolled to her side and sat up, placing his feet on the carpet and leaning back on his arms. The knit pants rode down on his hips, exposing his stomach, which was lean and flat except for a tiny swell above his navel.

"The only-child syndrome," he said sheepishly. "I never had to share my toys."

"Don't think of me as your toy." She looked away.

"I don't think of you that way."

"Alex, I don't know what to think."

"Something's happening to me, Katie. I don't always like it, but I've never felt this way about a woman."

"What do you want me to say?"

"Nothing. Just put up with me for a while."

"Until you can get me out of your system?"

"I'm not saying that."

"Maybe you should go."

"Yes, I will. Can we keep the possibilities open?"

She sat and drew up her legs, tugging her robe over her feet and resting her chin on her knees. "I guess they are open."

"No more weekend invitations," he said with undisguised regret. "No more coming on heavy. Just have dinner with me once in a while."

"You're a lonely bachelor who hates to eat by himself?"

"No, I just want to get to know you better."

"As my employer?"

"No, as your friend."

He kissed her good night at the door, a gentle, almost brotherly brush against her forehead, then her lips.

"I didn't even notice the garlic," he said softly.

Kate held up the urn, letting the ceiling light filter through it; she could see the outline of her fingers through the translucent porcelain. Under the black light it had appeared to be perfect, and the quality of the gilt and floral ornamentation made her determined to trace its origin. Instinct told her it was German, but the peculiar little curlicue mark on the bottom defied her best efforts to identify it. Alex's library was excellent, but she'd nearly exhausted the available sources. Maybe she'd have to consult a porcelain expert.

"Are you ready to leave?"

Alex came up the stairs, careful to warn her of his arrival by coughing as he came to the top step. No sane antiques dealer risked startling an employee holding a piece worth several thousand dollars.

"This urn is driving me crazy. Do you have any ideas about it?"

"It was part of a whole estate I bought. I'm leaning toward Russian. No luck with the books?"

"Not a glimmer. I'll be seeing that silly mark in my sleep."

"I'll call Pete Steiner tomorrow. If anyone can nail it down, he can."

"Is he a friend of yours?"

"I helped him find a Minton flask for his first book on English china. What are you doing for dinner?"

"I have plans. Sorry."

"So am I. I have to go to Candlebrook tomorrow. What about Wednesday? Can we have dinner together then?"

"All right."

It was a mistake not to say no. At work they were both extremely busy, and he seemed to avoid her, assigning her jobs that separated them. Even then, he was rarely far from her thoughts. She wasn't strong enough to look into those eyes over a candle-lit table and deny she wanted him as a lover. Saying yes to him would be easy; living with herself afterward wouldn't. His feelings might be sincere now, but what would happen when he tired of her? She wasn't sophisticated or worldly enough to have an affair and then continue to work for the man when it was over. A temporary romance with her boss could ruin her career; worse, it could break her heart.

Bill met her at a Chinese restaurant he'd discovered on a walking tour of Chinatown. Basement dining wasn't her favorite when it came to atmosphere, but the number of Chinese families eating there convinced her that the food was authentic. They shared chicken with cashew nuts and fish in a black-bean sauce, but she let him eat the major portion of both dishes.

"Tired?" he asked sympathetically as they cracked open the fortune cookies that came with their cups of Chinese tea.

"Maybe a little. I worked for hours trying to identify a porcelain urn and came up empty."

"My day was pretty good." He smiled, not self-conscious about letting her know about his successes. "Looks like I'll nail down that hotel-chain contract. Should keep the plant booming for quite a while."

"So there won't be any layoffs this summer?"

"Better. We may have to take on some temporaries."

From his description of the job, Kate was sure packing liver wasn't for her, but his quiet friendliness made the evening enjoyable. Really, he was a sweet man: modest, kind, cheerful, generous. Some woman was going to be very happy settling down with him and raising lovely children. She was almost sorry it wouldn't be her. The career role wasn't paradise on earth for any woman, and being pursued by a seductive employer was a no-win situation.

That evening Bill came to her apartment for the first time. He helped her finish Alex's Bordeaux, not asking why she had French wine in a refrigerator that contained only yogurt, juice, and carrots.

"I think I prefer beer," he said, setting the glass on an end table and leaning over to kiss her.

His lips were warm; his kisses were slow and easy.

"Sit on my lap here, honey," he urged, loosening his tie and the top button of his yellow permanent-press shirt. "I'd sure hate to get used to living in one of these dinky New York apartments."

"Less to clean," she suggested, moving onto his lap.

"You keep it nice."

His thighs were wide and solid, one of them easily accommodating her bottom. She felt like being kissed and cuddled, and snuggled against his broad chest with more contentment than passion. Big men were so comforting. Bill's gentleness gave her a soothing, secure glow. With only the dim light over the kitchen sink illuminating the room, the atmosphere was cozy. She wiggled closer and sighed, not minding when he fondled her breasts through the front of her pale blue rayon blouse.

"Nice," he said, kissing her cheek and pushing her skirt up on her thigh.

He seemed more interested than aroused, sliding his blunt fingers over her legs and patting her tummy—a gesture that only reminded her that days of starvation were the price of heavy restaurant dinners.

"For the first time I'm not in a hurry to get back to Iowa," he said.

"New York can be exciting," she agreed sleepily, letting her head droop against his chest.

"I'm finding that out. Does this couch turn into a bed?"

"Yes, but I don't think we're ready for that, Bill."

"Then I probably should go now," he said regretfully.

She didn't want him to go, not yet anyway, but she didn't want him to stay the night either.

"Tomorrow's a workday," Kate agreed.

"Darn it, I've got an appointment in Brooklyn first thing in the morning. My taxi expenses are going to be more than the plane fare at the rate I'm going." He kissed her soundly, then pushed her from his lap with a show of manly sacrifice.

"I had a nice time," she said at the door.

"I'm thinking of renting a car this weekend. Before I leave, I'd like to go to Atlantic City."

"It's a good idea to do all you can while you're on the East Coast."

"You wouldn't want to come with me? Separate rooms— my treat. I'm not trying to rush you."

81

"Sorry. I have an appointment Saturday morning. I can't depend on being free at any set time. But do go. You'll enjoy it."

"Without you? I doubt it. Maybe I'll just forget it."

"No, then you'll make me feel guilty!"

"Well, I was counting on one trip there. But I'll only go if you'll have a late supper with me Sunday night."

"I'll fix something for you here." She really enjoyed cooking when there was someone to share the meal.

"It's a deal!" He kissed her enthusiastically and left.

"It was a nice evening," she said aloud to herself when Bill was gone.

Alex wasn't the only man in the world, and he definitely wasn't the man to make her happy. The prospect of being a housewife in Nebraska had appalled her at eighteen, but that had been nearly ten years ago. Would it be so terrible to go back to the Midwest and create a happy, loving home?

Alex found it necessary to stay in Connecticut, missing their Wednesday dinner. Part of Kate was relieved, and she certainly wasn't lonely anymore. She saw Bill every evening, although he didn't come up to her apartment again. Wednesday they went to the top of the Empire State Building, something she would never have done alone. Thursday the Yankees were in town and the weather cooperated, giving them a balmy evening with only a slight breeze. It didn't matter to her that Detroit beat the New York team, but Bill seemed to see it as a vindication of the Midwest. Because his Friday afternoon was free of appointments, she convinced him to leave early for Atlantic City and take advantage of two evenings there.

"If I break the bank, we'll fly to Vegas and try our luck there," he told her on the phone, calling to say good-bye until Sunday and only half joking about his gambling expectations.

"Not many people come home big winners," she warned.

"Meeting you has already made me a big winner." His

laugh reassured her. "I have a week's salary in my pocket. When that's gone, I'll be back, even if it's tomorrow. You don't have to worry about me being foolish with money, honey."

Bill would never be foolish about anything. He would amble through life making sensible, safe decisions, extracting pleasure from ordinary things, not demanding a great deal. He wasn't fervently in love with life, but he liked the world and the people around him. He more than liked her. Being with him was good for her ego. He never challenged her ability or her right to forge ahead in her career; he quietly praised her knowledge and especially her "spunkiness" in coming to New York on her own. She was extremely fond of him.

With the Saturday-morning appointment shortening her weekend, she went home Friday intending to clean the apartment and do her hand laundry. There were worse things than a quiet evening at home catching up on little jobs. The phone was ringing when she unlocked her door.

"I just missed you at the gallery," Alex said.

"I had to pick up some groceries on the way home."

"Have you eaten?"

"No, but I really do need to stay home this evening and do some housecleaning."

"You're not angry because I canceled our dinner Wednesday?"

"No, of course not."

"My warehouse manager quit, and it hasn't been easy trying to replace him. I didn't want to leave until things were settled."

"You found someone?"

"Yes, he's a former dealer. Retired, and hated being on the sidelines. He'll probably only work a few years because his wife wants to live in Florida, but I'm lucky to have him."

"Your week went well, then?"

"No. I didn't see you."

83

"Alex . . ."

"Come to my place for dinner."

"I don't think so."

"Just dinner."

"I . . ."

"We have a lot to talk about—business."

"I have an appointment tomorrow morning. We could meet afterward for lunch."

"I'm tied up tomorrow. I really should talk to you tonight."

"I know, it's not a nine-to-five job." The resignation in her voice wasn't at all what she was feeling.

"Still, dinner is a request, not an order. You don't have to come, Kate."

"I suppose I should."

"That's not exactly leaping at my invitation, but I'll settle for it. Seven thirty all right?"

"Yes, I'll be there then."

"I can come for you."

"No, thanks, I'll get there."

She did have dozens of questions, business questions, to ask him. When he was gone, her responsibilities were heavy. Tomorrow's appointment was with a decorator who was involved in the restoration of an eighteenth-century house. Alex had worked with him in the past and could tell her what to expect. Really, it would be foolish not to confer with the head of the gallery before her Saturday meeting.

Liar, she thought vehemently, you would debate whether a snail or a worm can crawl faster if it meant being with Alex! Admit you have a king-size crush on the man!

Maybe seeing him more often would help her get over her infatuation. He was always breezing in and out like a knight preparing to do battle with a dragon. Naturally he seemed exciting. No doubt the ladies left behind in their castles had felt the same way until their warriors came home for the winter and inflicted their bad humors onto the domestic

84

scene. If she saw Alex more frequently, he wouldn't seem so intriguing. Familiarity breeds contempt; this good old saying had a lot of truth in it. She had romanticized the upper strata of the antiques business for such a long time, it wasn't surprising that Alex seemed like some kind of hero: the wheeler-dealer who was always suave, sophisticated, and debonair. She had to remember: he was no different from the shop owner at an Omaha show who had tried to talk her into selling a lovely old butter churn for half its value. Success in the trade meant being shrewd, calculating, opportunistic, and—Oh, damn it, who was she trying to kid now? Nothing she knew about Alex tarnished his image. He was honest, hardworking, considerate, intelligent, and fair. And he had all but promised he wouldn't pull rank to try to seduce her.

Wondering how Bill would fare in Atlantic City, she wished she had gone with him. Life in the fast lane was more complicated than she had ever imagined.

Tempted to show up wearing jeans and a sweatshirt, she couldn't quite bring herself to do it and dressed instead in tailored navy slacks and a lavender knit top. The weather had turned warm, but she grabbed a bulky white sweater on her way out just in case it was chilly later. Of course, she planned to get home early in the evening.

Alex opened the door wearing faded jeans and a red tank top, his bare shoulders and arms more muscular than she'd suspected. His bare feet, which sank into the pile of the carpet, looked white and vulnerable compared with the tanned complexion of his face. Why should she feel that the absence of shoes made their meeting more intimate? She'd been fifteen before willingly wearing shoes in the summer.

"You're really going to be impressed with my feast," he said with his mocking half smile.

"Let me guess. Steak."

"Wrong."

"Hamburgers?"

"You underestimate me. It's all laid out. I hope you drink German beer."

He guided her toward the kitchen where high bar stools surrounded an island counter which also served as a casual dining table. The display of food could only have come from a delicatessen.

"Pastrami, corned beef, dill pickles. You like exotic food. Here's native New York à la carte."

"I was sure you'd broil a steak."

"Too boring for you. Look at these: stuffed cabbage, smoked salmon, rye bread with caraway seeds, cold tongue, coleslaw."

"You have enough food for a week."

"You're welcome to stay as long as it takes you to finish it."

"You'd better be planning to eat quite a bit yourself."

"I don't mind corned beef on rye with a little potato salad. The cheesecake is in the fridge."

"That will make you fat!"

"Not if I exercise enough." His conversation was innocent, but the glint in his eyes would make a swinger blush. "How was your week without me?"

"Very busy. Do you ever stay home and mind the store?"

"Things go pretty smoothly without me. My real genius lies in choosing good employees."

"Does it now?" She accepted a large paper plate and began helping herself from the overly ample buffet. "I have to agree that Nancy and Blanche are wonders—and Jack is very efficient too."

He wasn't touching her, but she could feel him standing behind her, so close the warmth of his body seemed to radiate over hers.

"Try a pickle." He reached around her, brushing her arm with his, the hairs tickling her skin. The fat green object he forked onto her plate had begun life as a three-inch cucumber. "Garlic dills. I'm having one too."

"That's of absolutely no consequence to me," she said coldly, remembering how the spicy spaghetti sauce had tainted her breath.

"We do have a lot to talk about."

"We certainly do," she agreed. "That urn is driving me crazy. It's as if I've seen a picture of it somewhere but where, where, where?"

"We'll say it contained the ashes of Catherine the Great's lover and sell it for a fortune."

"Which lover? She had the whole palace guard."

"Vladimir Pavlovitch."

"There's no such person! You made that up." She nibbled a slice of pastrami. "The period isn't even right."

"That's not why people buy antiques. They buy mystery, legend, glamour, intrigue." He put half a container of potato salad on his plate. "Did you know the Indians used to eat the hearts of enemies to get their courage?"

"Alex! Not while we're eating." She sat back on her stool and pushed away the plate.

"Sorry, just making a point. I'd rather eat sand than heart or liver. People buy the romance of the past when they buy antiques. I sold a shabby, rickety desk with worm holes for a huge price because the original owner in the nineteenth century had committed suicide when a woman rejected him."

"That's morbid."

"No, it's not. Don't you think dying for love is romantic?"

"More like silly." She felt like pouting.

"Then you've never been in love?"

"Of course I have!" Or had she? Leaving Randy had hurt, but in retrospect she didn't much like him.

"Oh?" His broad smile dared her to reveal all.

"You're the authority. You must know all about love."

"It's next of kin to insanity! Adult men start acting like demented teenagers, and women . . ."

"Women what?"

"Have another piece of stuffed cabbage."

"I haven't eaten this one. What do women do when they're in love?"

"I'm not an expert in that field."

"You need to call in a consultant, then?"

"I'm not consumed by curiosity, and I certainly don't anticipate any profits from that particular information."

"So profits are the most important thing?"

"No." He sounded irritated now.

"But a person would have to be crazy to fall in love?"

"It does bring on the same symptoms as mental illness: neglect of work, obsessive behavior—"

"Extreme happiness?" she interrupted.

"More like temporary euphoria. But no high lasts forever."

"You sound like a true cynic. I'm beginning to believe you've been badly burned."

"Oh, no! Don't look for some tragic love affair in my past. My life-style isn't compatible with heavy romance."

"Have you ever worked the show circuit?" she asked, deliberately changing the subject.

"Sure. Before I started the warehouse in Candlebrook, most of my income came from doing shows. The gallery came later. You're not eating much."

"I guess I'm not very hungry."

"Too many dinner dates this week?"

"Something like that." She tried to flash a coy smile in his direction, but all he picked up was the challenge in her voice.

"It's none of my business, of course," he said dryly. "Unless it interferes with your work."

"I can't imagine why it would."

"You may have to do some traveling. I forgot to ask if you have a passport."

"I do."

"You've been abroad, then?"

88

"Only once. A whirlwind tour of England and Scotland sponsored by an alumni group."

They finished the meal with only a few spurts of desultory small talk.

"Cheesecake?" he asked, beginning to stuff the remains of the delicatessen feast into plastic bags.

"No, thank you."

"I've worked with this decorator Purvis before," he said when they were sitting at opposite sides of the living room. "He'll try to wear you down on every price. His tactic is to nag until you lower the price just to put an end to his haggling."

"I won't let him get away with it," she promised.

"Just start the bidding high so you have room to negotiate. I know who his client is, and he'll insist on high quality. Purvis will be working with several dealers, but I think he especially wants a Massachusetts highboy. We have one, but he's going to have to pay our price."

"Are you sure you don't want to work with him yourself?"

"No, that's why I hired you. You can handle him, can't you?" He was stretched out on the couch like a lazy tiger, yawning and flexing, tempting her to watch the play of muscles in his bare arms and shoulders. What she couldn't handle was the stab of sheer longing in her own body, a continuous ache to touch and be touched that was generated by being near him.

Rising slowly, stretching his whole body sensuously, he strolled toward the music case, unlocking it with a key he took from his pocket.

"I lock it so my cleaning woman won't get overly zealous and try dusting them," he explained, taking out one of the newer-looking instruments. "My first guitar. American, twentieth century."

He pulled a footstool close to the chair where she was sitting with her legs tucked under her.

89

"I don't play very often at parties. My repertoire isn't very large, but with the right kind of audience I do improvise."

After a few tentative strums he began.

"In Hartford town where I was born,
There was a plumb maid dwelling. . . ."

"I know that tune," she said accusingly when he'd finished the bawdy verse, more funny than shocking. "But those words have to be original."

"Now you know my secret." He turned, resting his arm against her knee. "I like to update folk songs with my own words."

"Then 'Oh, Katie, My Love' isn't a real ballad?"

"Only the lady's name was changed. I don't know any Mollys." He started humming, then broke into a lively song.

"Oh, Katie, my love, I would I could—"

"I don't like that version at all!"

She bounded out of the chair, feeling irrationally close to tears. The song had been so lovely when he'd said "woo you." Their business discussion was over, and she wanted to run away from that sensual voice, the suggestive verses, and the undisguised desire in his eyes.

"You're angry. I'm sorry." He quickly laid aside the instrument and followed her to the door. "Don't go yet."

"I think I should."

"Do you want to leave because you don't trust me—or because you don't trust yourself?"

"I know what I'm going to do. Leave."

"Stay a while longer. I promise to behave."

He wasn't touching her, but his words, like invisible ropes, stretched around her ummoving body.

"Please." He lowered his head, brushing his lips over her forehead and the lids of her eyes.

All she had to do to break free of the bonds that held her prisoner was to reach out and touch him. Clenching her hands at her sides, she was determined not to give in to the insistent clamoring of her heart. She didn't want Alex Gilbert! She didn't want to bury herself in his arms and revel in the lean hardness of his body and feel him moving against her and . . .

His kiss was savage, shattering the icy statue in his arms, demanding honesty from her response and receiving it as she writhed against him like a woman possessed by demons. His hands kneaded her shoulders, her arms, her back, and her buttocks while she clung to him, wanting his assault to go on and on. There was no way she could deny her desire to make love with him. His breath was ragged in her ear, and her own heart was thudding like a war drum.

"Katie." He gathered her roughly against him, trapping one of her legs between his. "Katie."

Her back was against the door, and her hands were doing what they'd done countless times in her imagination, caressing the warm skin of his back under the tank top, feeling the knobby ridge of his spine, sliding along the waistband of his jeans.

The knocking noise was so close to her ear, she thought it came from her own head. Alex swore fluently under his breath and released her. He stood for a moment, breathing heavily to restore his composure.

"How can someone be at your door? You have more security in your building than the White House."

"Neighbors can drop by anytime without buzzing," he said grimly. "They're already in the building."

She retreated across the room, dropping into a chair and picking up the guitar to cover her agitation. "Do you have to answer?"

"No, but I might as well."

A pale, neatly dressed man with an overcoat over his arm smiled apologetically when Alex opened the door. "Hate to bother you, Alex, but all I've been able to get the last hour was your answering machine. I checked downstairs on my way out, and they said you were in."

"What can I do for you?" Alex asked. His voice almost sounded normal.

"My wife's mother is extremely ill. We're on our way to Providence. Would you mind feeding our cats for a couple of days? My wife won't trust the doorman, since she came home from Mexico last year and found their water dishes nearly empty."

"Sure, I'll be glad to." Alex took his neighbor's key. "I'm sorry about your mother-in-law."

"Thanks." The man didn't linger.

"Bad timing," Alex said when the door was shut. "But they're nice people. She sent me chicken soup when I had the flu last year."

"Did it make you feel better?"

"It had little green specks in it, so I didn't try it."

He stood under the arch between the foyer and the living room, one hand on his hip and the other behind his head. He didn't look comfortable.

"Alex." Her legs were unsteady, and she felt like a survivor of a disaster who'd narrowly missed being a victim.

"It wasn't a good idea anyway," he said with resignation.

"I'm sorry."

"Do not apologize." He said each word with chilling intensity. "I don't intend to."

"Write it off as chemistry?" she asked timidly, without meeting his stare.

"A near explosion."

"You don't mind if I leave now?"

"Do you mind if I don't take you home?"

"No, of course not."

She stumbled around, somehow finding her purse and sweater, wishing he would move away from the arch so he wasn't blocking her retreat.

"I can't think of a clever exit line," she said awkwardly, standing ten feet away, waiting for him to move.

"You don't need one." He moved aside, letting her leave in silence.

CHAPTER FIVE

Only Saturday's triumph of a big sale to the decorator gave her the courage to face Alex Monday morning. Agreeing to have dinner at his apartment had been sheer folly! The business they'd discussed could easily have been handled in a short phone conversation.

Letting herself in through the private entrance, she smoothed her tailored navy linen dress, determined to behave like a model of professional competence—and nothing else. He had made his views on romance painfully clear: love was a trap, a snare he wanted to avoid at any cost. Well, Mr. Alex Gilbert was safe with her; she certainly didn't have any designs on his bachelor freedom. And he could forget his seductive tactics too. She wouldn't be lulled into another scene like the one by his door.

Grimly steeling herself for a confrontation with her employer, she practically snapped at Jack Fisher when he said good morning on the stairs. Stopping a moment to apologize for her abruptness, she received the unwelcome message that Mr. Gilbert wanted to see her in his office.

"Good morning," she said formally, standing in the doorway to his office.

"Come in and shut the door." His manner wasn't exactly cordial either. "You did pretty well with Purvis."

Pretty well, indeed! "Thank you."

"You gave him quite a bargain on the candle stand, but I guess we'll come out all right on the console table." He was seated behind his desk, paying more attention to a pile of papers than to her.

"I stayed within the guidelines you gave me. He's definitely interested in the highboy."

"Don't feel hurt. I'm not criticizing." He looked up and stared at her through narrowed eyes. "Purvis is a pain in the rear. I'm glad not to have to deal with him."

"He was very pleasant to me."

"I'll bet he was." He stood and regarded her with a peculiar expression.

"I fed the cats," he said.

"Oh?" She looked over at his Toulouse-Lautrec, but the earthy-looking woman with rusty hair did nothing to lighten her mood.

"My neighbors' cats. People who travel a lot shouldn't keep pets."

"You don't like animals?"

"I didn't say that."

She'd never heard him sound so touchy.

"You implied it."

"You have a habit of only hearing what you want to hear," he said dryly.

The unfairness of his accusation stung.

"Why are you angry with me?"

"I'm not angry!" he protested, the force of his words convincing her he was.

"If that's all you want, I have a lot to do upstairs."

"I know exactly what you have to do, and it isn't urgent enough to send you flying out of here. Are you afraid of me, Kate?"

"Certainly not!" She hated the hot feeling that surged to her face. "But you're not exactly congenial this morning."

"I'm sorry. I'll be congenial." He sounded as begrudging as a miser agreeing to make a large contribution. "Can we go over this week's schedule?"

"Of course." She didn't like his black suit; it was too som-

95

ber and dreary, even though the effect was softened by a strand of hair that fell rebelliously forward on his forehead.

She listened attentively as he flipped the pages of his daily calendar and read the parts of the schedule that concerned her. Most of what he told her was already written in her date book on the third-floor desk assigned to her. Blanche was a whiz at keeping the staff informed.

"And Saturday evening we have a dinner party," he said in the same flat tone of voice.

"We have a dinner party?"

"It'll be formal—wear a long dress if you have one. I'll come for you around eight."

"Just a minute, Mr. Gilbert. You can't just assume I'll go to a party with you on Saturday."

"Contacts are important in this business. I did assume you understood that."

"Why are you acting this way?"

"I am not acting any way!"

"Then why are you shouting at me?"

"I'm not shouting." His voice became soft but sullen. "I'm a very busy businessman trying to lay out the week's schedule for my administrative assistant."

"You have every right to fill Monday through Friday, but I should have some choice on Saturday night." She was amazed at her own nerve; her job might be hanging on a thread, but she didn't deserve such high-handed treatment.

He moved away and stood by the window with his back turned for a long moment.

"I'm sorry. I'm not in a very good mood this morning." He faced her and moved closer. "Can we start over? Good morning, Ms. Bevan. How was your weekend?"

"Very nice, thank you, Mr. Gilbert." She would play his game, even if she doubted his sincerity.

"I tried to call you Sunday. Several times."

"I was in and out all day. I must have missed you."

96

"I did get an answer in the evening, but my motto is: if a man answers, hang up."

"You were the wrong number?" Bill had picked up the phone because she was busy with the sautéed scallops, her treat after his successful weekend in Atlantic City.

"I wanted to say I was sorry about Saturday evening," he said grudgingly.

"Please don't. You tell me not to apologize."

"I don't know you well enough to inflict my bawdy verses on you."

"I rather enjoyed them," she admitted a little sheepishly.

"That's something. There's no reason why you should believe me, but the dinner party is strictly business. You realize how important it is to know people in this business."

"You're the one people need to know. I'm just an assistant."

"You'll be a lot more valuable to me when you know more of our clients."

"I have plans for Saturday night. Tentative plans, anyway."

"How tentative?" He sat on the edge of the desk, swinging one leg but no more relaxed than she was.

Bill's work in New York was done; the flight home was scheduled for Sunday morning. How could she refuse to spend his last evening in New York with him?

When she didn't answer immediately, Alex went on: "I don't know how seriously you take your job, Kate, but I am disappointed in one thing. You don't seem to be making any effort to get acquainted with my clients. It's not enough to go to parties with me. You need to socialize."

There was just enough truth in his accusation to humiliate her. She wasn't comfortable with people like Myra Webster and her friends, and they were important to Alex's gallery trade.

"Maybe I don't belong here," she said, miserable.

"Don't be silly!" He stepped forward and rested both

hands on her shoulders. "You're a tremendous asset. I couldn't have handled Purvis any better myself. In fact, I often have an almost uncontrollable urge to boot him out."

The important thing was not to cry. She wouldn't let Alex see her weeping!

"Don't look like that," he said, sounding a little stricken himself. "I didn't intend to hurt your feelings."

"You haven't," she protested stiffly.

"But you do see what I mean about getting to know clients and potential clients?"

"Yes." She wasn't shy around most people; why did the ones she met at New York parties intimidate her? "Is this party terribly important?"

"It's important to me that you go."

"All right." She sighed and avoided his eyes.

How could she expect Bill to believe that going to a dinner party with Alex was only business?

She told him that evening, after the movie, as they strolled along enjoying the fine weather.

"I'd like to tell that slave driver a few things," he said.

"He did warn me before I took the job that it would require more than working nine to five."

"The question is, how much more?" Bill squeezed her against his side and walked slower.

"I imagine there won't be as many social events in the summer. It's just bad luck that this one coincides with your last evening here."

"Not as bad as you think," he said with a grin. "I won enough in Atlantic City to treat myself to a non-expense-account week in Manhattan. I have vacation time coming, so I've arranged to take next week. Just tell me Sunday night is mine."

"That's wonderful, Bill."

It was. Seeing him go back to Iowa would be like losing a best friend. Even a short delay was welcome.

"Any chance you can get some time off during my big week?" he asked.

"I'd love to, but I've been with the gallery such a short time, I'm afraid to ask. I'll have all of August off when it closes for a month."

"That could fit into my plans very nicely," he said with a secretive smile.

Saturday came too soon. Spending every evening with Bill had put her way behind on everyday chores, but she agreed to meet him for lunch in the park. They frolicked like kids, running barefoot in the prickly grass, absorbing the sun until their faces were bright pink. Her hair always lightened in the summer, and she wondered if the two of them would look like brother and sister at the end of the season.

Fun in the sun was forgotten when she got back to her apartment. Her face was a shiny beet-red that defied all efforts to subdue it with makeup. Worse, her only sophisticated long dress was a tangerine shade that clashed horribly with her sunburn. Low in back, it revealed pale wintery skin that made her reddened arms and face look even worse. Nothing about the evening looked promising. Undoubtedly, all the other women at the party would be wearing fur miniskirts or transparent harem pants or little oriental numbers that were slit up to their armpits. She dressed with dread, feeling caught in a no-win situation, unable to do the expected thing because she didn't know what it was.

At least the orange gown did marvelous things for her figure. Her breasts swelled above the nipped-in waist, and her hips looked seductively slim under the graceful silky sweep of the skirt. An unusual dress, it would have been flattering if her skin had been its usual fair shade. With her hair piled precariously on her head because she hadn't had time to have it done professionally, and with her sunburn beginning to smart, she could only hope for a short evening.

Alex came to the door, presenting her with a little nosegay of white rosebuds that she anchored in her hair. They had seen little of each other all week, and she wondered, not for the first time, whether he had deliberately avoided her.

"What happened to your face?" he asked, slipping her white, silk-fringed shawl—another antique treasure— around her shoulders.

"Just a little sun. I burn easily."

"You look like you've been following a camel caravan across the Sahara. Are you in pain?"

The biggest pain was the one he was causing.

"I'm fine. Shall we go?" She wanted to say, shall we get this over with?

"Don't be afraid to talk to people," Alex said softly in the foyer of the graciously decorated apartment overlooking Central Park.

"I'm not!" She felt like shaking him; nothing hindered a smooth flow of conversation more than being ordered to talk.

The women's dresses ran to brocades and silks, and their average age was seventy. The few younger couples seemed aloof, keeping to their own small group, and Kate was in no mood to win friends. The furnishings—genuine Colonial American pieces mixed with extremely tasteful reproductions—gave the rooms the look of museum settings.

"They're quite a bit older than you," Kate observed after meeting the Beldings, their hosts.

"Mrs. Belding went to school with my mother," he said. "Was your friend upset with you for breaking your date?"

"Not at all. He's a very good sport."

"That's nice." His tone made it clear that he didn't want to believe her.

The whole evening was a performance on her part. She pretended to be enthralled by one guest's account of a trip to Africa in 1964, then listened to a woman endlessly extolling her grandchildren's virtues to a captive group. When her host, Mr. Belding, insisted on showing Kate a collection of Vargas paintings in his den, she remembered her father's saying about snow on the roof not indicating the flame was out in the furnace. When the old goat patted her bottom, it was all she could do not to throw some well-deserved cold water on his fire. If this was Alex's idea of socializing, she would rather be like her great-great-uncle Fred, who was born, lived, and died in an apartment over the family grocery store, venturing forth for only two reasons in his adult life: to register for the World War I draft and to exchange his teeth for dentures. Maybe reclusiveness was hereditary; maybe she was destined to end up as a hermit, surrounded by the debris of years of antiques picking, as suspicious of people as the doll seller who had tried to con her. None of this would have occurred to her before she had met Alex!

Alex was immensely popular with all age-groups, welcomed by the exclusive little knot of younger guests and courted by the older ones. How many of them had eligible daughters or even granddaughters? Kate wondered, not feeling good about herself and disliking her own suspicions. She toyed with her evening bag, a really spectacular creation covered with tiny metallic beads in shades of copper, silver, and dark blue, and was surprised when Alex came up behind her and put his hands on her arms.

"Have you been to the buffet?" he asked.

"No, not yet." Pheasant under glass wouldn't tempt her tonight.

"Come along with me."

The generous spread was what she imagined a Scandinavian smorgasbord to be, with emphasis on seafood and cold meats. The herring with sour cream and onions tempted her, as did salmon molded in the shape of a fish. Alex helped himself to sliced roast beef and ham, but she sampled the Danish meatballs and pâté. An assortment of fresh fruit and cheese gave the meal a nice finish, but her gourmet instincts were dulled; she picked at the food on her plate without enthusiasm.

101

"Am I spoiling your appetite?" Alex asked solemnly, standing beside her as they ate without benefit of a table.

"No, the food is very good."

"Forget what I said before," he said, watching her face closely. "Don't make hard work out of socializing. You're lovely, and people like you."

Not the people you know, she wanted to say, but instead stared at her plate.

"I don't like to force myself on people," she said.

"You're not." He sounded irritated again, then repeated more gently, "You're not doing that."

Was it sunburn or Alex that made her feel feverish? He stayed close to her for the rest of the evening, going out of his way to include her in conversations. When she made a remark that amused an insurance executive and his wife, he beamed at her like a fond parent but made her feel like a performing seal. His willingness to leave early came as a great relief.

"Would you mind stopping at the gallery on the way home?" he asked. "I had a file laid out to work on at home tomorrow, but I forgot it."

They went in through the front entrance, Alex hurrying to the phone to give his code number to the security service. Being in the dimly lit gallery at night was a new and slightly spooky experience, and she could imagine the ghosts of former owners hovering over the possessions they had treasured in life.

"Coming up with me?" Alex asked.

She had no intention of staying alone in the salesroom.

The second and third floors were dark except for lights at the top of each flight of stairs, but Alex found what he wanted on his desk without turning on the overhead lights. Waiting for him, she edged closer to the Art Deco sculpture in the reception room, enjoying the shadowy nudes in the gray gloom, seeing the glint of metal limbs against the heavy blackness of the marble base.

"Do you like it?" Alex's voice was a soft caress behind her.

Half turning, she moved into his arms without thinking about it, parting her lips under the gentle caress of his mouth. Papers rustled as they fell from his folder and hit the floor, the sound magnified by the late-night stillness. He kissed her cheeks, her chin, the lobes of her ears, brushing his lashes against her eyelids, then kissing them shut.

"I'm breaking my promise," he whispered hoarsely.

"Promise?" Her memory was gone; only the here and now existed.

"I said you'd be safe in the gallery. Do you want to be safe, Katie?"

"No." She blurted out the truth, the muscles constricting in her throat. "I want you."

Her evening bag fell to the floor, as did her shoes when he lifted her in his arms. She moaned softly when she found his neck with her lips and smothered it with nipping little kisses. Drunk on the scent of his skin, she hardly noticed as he carried her down the poorly lit stairs to the back room of the gallery, stopping in front of an Empire sofa longer than his length. The night lights from the salesroom barely penetrated this recessed alcove, and he let her slide to her feet in the circle of his arms.

"I just bought this sofa," he said softly. "You can research it Monday."

"Yes, I will."

His words didn't really register. All her senses were focused on his hands, which were stroking her neck and trailing down her spine.

"Does your sunburn hurt?"

"I'd forgotten it."

Everything was forgotten: all the sane, logical reasons not to become emotionally involved with her employer. With the suddenness of a dam bursting she blocked out misgivings

103

and insecurities, her mind open only to the thrilling sensations of his lips on her face, his hands on her body.

"Ohhhh." A moan of ecstasy escaped as he unzipped her gown and let it slide to a heap around her feet.

Her skin was hungry for his, and she reached for his shirt buttons without considering consequences; fumbling to undo them, she was grateful when he struggled free of his jacket, shirt, and tie and let them fall where they would. Pushing her fingers through his hair, she swayed forward, shivering when he slid the straps of her slip over her shoulders and let the garment join the tangle of clothing at her feet. He released her bra and embraced her, flattening her breasts against the harder expanse of his chest, murmuring into her hair, exploring the trembling length of her body with gently kneading hands.

"You feel so good," he crooned, taking the weight of her breasts into his hands and bending to taste each one in turn.

As their eyes became accustomed to the dim light, they feasted all their senses, at first tentatively and then heatedly exploring each other's body. They stripped off their remaining garments and held each other close, reveling in their abandonment to passion.

Rubbing her legs against his, she loved the feel of his body hair against her smoother limbs, loved the swells of muscle under her fingers and the firm roundness of his buttocks. Their need to touch was a hunger that cried for satisfaction, a thirst that required oceans to quench. They were like actors in a play, going through each motion with great deliberation because they knew what the conclusion would be. When he became more demanding, she savored it, climbing with him to a peak of urgency.

A little voice told her this shouldn't be happening, but his gentle whispers drowned it out. Lowering her to the sofa, he hovered over her, raining soft kisses on her breasts, parting her legs to stoke a fire that was already a major conflagration.

The upholstery under her naked back was slick with age, and Alex struggled to fit his knees beside her on the narrow width. Grasping at him to help, she heard the aged framework creak. Then with a deep sigh that was relief as well as passion, he penetrated deep within her, capturing her in a rhythm as primitive as the beginning of life and as new as the moment.

The ancient wood groaned in protest, but neither heard it, deafened by the roar of their senses and the pounding of their bodies.

Lost in the newness of her response, Kate marveled at what an empty wasteland her life had been till then, and loved Alex so much she wanted the two of them to become one person. The loud protest of an abused spring fell on deaf ears, and a weak wooden leg, a fraction of an inch different in length from its companions, cracked in protest.

A rush of heat skyrocketed through her, bombarding her with burst after burst of glorious sensations, while Alex shuddered convulsively, crushing her with his weight to save himself from plunging sideways to the floor. Their world rocked as a greater cracking noise startled them, the splintering of the fragile front leg accomplishing what he'd tried to prevent, spilling them to the gritty wooden floor of the workroom.

"Oh, Alex, we broke it!" she cried in distress.

"I don't care!" He was laughing happily, rolling on his back and pulling her on top of him. "You're wonderful! I don't care!"

He pressed her face against his, grinding their lips together until she squirmed for breath.

"You're wonderful," he repeated, kissing her swollen lips more tenderly, touching the tip of her nose with his tongue. "Will you ever forgive me for breaking my promise?"

"There's nothing to forgive."

It was true. She had wanted Alex as much as he wanted her, and had given herself with years of stored-up passion.

Maybe someday she would regret their lovemaking, but at this moment her contentment overruled all her former doubts. She loved him; later she would worry about whether he loved her.

"Ohhh." He moaned deeply, squeezed her intimately, then moaned again.

"Is something wrong?" She nuzzled the hollow of his neck, inhaling the heady scent of musk and cuddling against his warm body.

"I'm trying to think of a way to explain that broken leg to Jack."

They laughed sheepishly, rising reluctantly to their feet.

"We'd better take a look," he said, switching on the overhead light.

The slender leg was shattered beyond repair, showing raw splinters where it had split completely. Kate's preservationist instincts assailed her; a hundred and seventy years ago a fine craftsman had fashioned that leg. She looked at Alex, expecting to see anger or regret in his face. Instead he was looking at her, his eyes half hooded and his mouth twisted into an odd little smile.

"Do you think he'll believe a mouse did it?" he asked.

They laughed until her eyes teared and he got a cramp in his side. They fell into each other's arms.

"You won't be laughing tomorrow," she warned.

"No, but I'll remember how beautiful you look right now, and that will be some compensation."

"Just some?"

"A whole lot." He switched off the light and gathered her into his arms.

CHAPTER SIX

Awaking in her own bed with her cheek burrowed into the pillow, Kate smiled dreamily, enjoying the luxury of remembering. Last night had been the wildest, craziest night of her life; she still couldn't believe their lovemaking had shattered the leg of an Empire sofa. The piece had needed work, particularly reupholstering, but their frenzied movements must have weakened a flaw in the wood. The leg could be replaced, and Alex would know a craftsman skillful enough to make detection almost impossible, but he would lose money on the repaired piece. Ethics would require that he point out the new leg to potential buyers, and flawed antiques brought lower prices.

Stretching flat on her back, she hugged her arms across the front of her lacy yellow nightgown, forgetting about the sofa leg as she relived every moment with Alex. What time had it been when he brought her home? Still floating on a cloud of happiness, she hadn't bothered to look. If he'd come into the apartment, he might be there beside her now, reaching for her, wanting her as she wanted him. Fumbling on the end table that did double duty as a nightstand, she found the travel alarm she'd forgotten to wind and then her wristwatch, which showed her it was indeed late in the morning. At home in Butterfield her mother would be through singing in the church choir and would be hanging the bright blue robe back in the music-room closet. Dad would be greeting people as they left the sanctuary, never suspecting that the whole congregation knew the ushers sneaked down to the kitchen for a cup of coffee during the sermon. It was sinfully late to be lying in bed, but she couldn't find anything wrong with feeling so content.

Did Alex feel the same way? She stretched lazily but was less comfortable thinking about his reaction to their lovemaking. He'd wanted it, urged it, probably planned it, but did it mean as much to him as it did to her? She felt cherished, desired, even exalted, but men could be so casual about sex. Not Alex, she kept trying to convince herself; but she was living for the ring of her phone, some tangible sign that his life was changed too.

His call didn't come. Late in the afternoon Bill coaxed her away from the apartment, insisting he couldn't go back to Iowa without walking through Greenwich Village with her. He acted like a typical tourist, greatly impressed that Aaron Burr and Mark Twain had once lived there. She got a blister on her heel and found a coarse black hair in her saffron-flavored rice at dinner. For the first time in her life she sent a restaurant dish back, not appreciating the flush on Bill's face when she refused a replacement and insisted on having the waiter subtract the item from the bill. They ordered a second pitcher of sangria, drinking the red wine punch so fast the room seemed to spin a little when they made their way out to the street.

On Monday Alex left on a buying trip to New England, leaving a message for Kate with Blanche. She was supposed to send the sofa out for repairs.

"Did he say anything about the Christie's auction?" Kate asked, trying to sound normal and businesslike.

"Only that he'll call you tonight. And be sure to phone the Petersons about that secretary-bookcase. Also, Mr. Purvis wants you to arrange for delivery of the highboy, and his client wants a globe for the library that shows the world before 1900."

"I'll run that through the computer," Kate said wearily, "but I don't recall one in the Candlebrook stock."

How could she feel so exhausted even before the gallery opened for the morning? She and Bill had made an early evening of it. He had wanted to come in and take care of her heel so it wouldn't get infected, but after he described what trainers did to athletes' blisters, she invented an excuse to send him home. Every time they were together, she was more impressed with his kindliness and good nature. He was totally trustworthy, generous to a fault, and considerate even when she didn't deserve it. He surprised her by coming to the gallery at noon, and she realized that a pleasant lunch in his company was just what she needed.

The phone was ringing when she got home from a movie with Bill, kissing him good night in the lobby because she was genuinely exhausted.

"Kate?" Alex's voice was caressing, but her disappointment in not hearing from him sooner nullified its effect.

"Yes."

"Sorry I didn't call you before this. It's been one hectic day. I just got back to the motel."

She didn't ask where he was. His neatly typed schedule for the week was posted on a corkboard in the gallery workroom.

"You didn't need to check in. Everything went smoothly today, but the sofa will take at least ten weeks. He's really behind on work."

"I suppose I should be grateful it's not ten months."

"I'm sorry the leg broke," she said stiffly.

His soft laugh gave her goose bumps. "I'm not."

"Purvis wants the highboy," she said.

"I thought he would."

"He also wants a globe, pre-1900. The computer didn't show one in stock."

"The computer's right. I'll try to find one. Stall him until I get back."

109

"When will that be?"

"Probably not before next Monday. I hope to hit a couple of weekend auctions."

"Well, everything is under control here." Her voice seemed to be sticking in her throat.

"I don't doubt it."

A moment later they hung up. It would have been better if he hadn't called at all. She hadn't expected an avowal of undying love; she did yearn for some word, some sign, that she was more to him than an employee. Even if Saturday night had been a casual fling for him, couldn't he throw her some crumb of affection? Nothing he'd said or done made her hope for a lifetime commitment, but his casual attitude was devastating. More than ever, she felt out of place in his brittle, sophisticated world. People she knew spoke their minds and didn't pretend to be anything they weren't.

Her eyes were swimming with tears when she replaced the phone receiver. What a fool she was to dream about a special place in Alex's life! She didn't hate him for making love to her, but she was terribly hurt because he acted as if it had never happened. Everything she'd read about single men on the prowl came back to haunt her, and she felt like a prize fool. Regardless of what the slick women's magazines said, she felt like a little hick from Nebraska who'd been had by a city swinger.

Work kept her occupied, but Bill helped more, meeting her every evening after work, waiting patiently on Tuesday when a phone problem made it impossible to activate the security system until the repairman came. Wednesday evening they saw the Mets play, and Thursday he asked if he could spend the night with her.

"I know I'm rushing you," he said with an apologetic grin, "but my time here is running out."

"Bill, our friendship means so much to me. I'm not sure we should jeopardize it."

She wouldn't make the same mistake twice; things would

never be the same with Alex. How could she think of him as just an employer after making love with him? She couldn't put her fondness for Bill to a test.

"We're more than friends," Bill argued persuasively. "I think I'm falling in love with you, Kate."

"I'm not sure you should. My job here is important to me, Bill. You're going home soon."

"Not till Sunday evening."

They were sitting on her couch, pretending to watch an evening TV show even though neither had the slightest idea what was happening in the story. Curled in the crook of his arm, Kate felt comfortable and secure. She didn't resist when he softly kissed her lips, but his hand felt heavy and hard groping at the front of her pink and white striped blouse. It wasn't a lack of gentleness on his part; rather, her body felt stiff and rigid, unyielding under his well-intentioned stroking. If she could forget Alex, Bill might be a marvelous lover; unfortunately, the complications of sex were the last thing she needed right now. When he bent toward her, his kiss was sweet on her lips, but her only reaction was a listless annoyance.

"I know when a girl's not in the mood," he said without resentment. "But I'm not going to take no for an answer forever."

Friday night she canceled their date, pleading a throbbing headache. It wasn't a fib; her forehead felt as if an iron band were tightening over her eyes. She felt so miserable that she got into bed as soon as she returned from work, unplugging the phone so she wouldn't be awakened by its piercing ring.

When Bill urged her to play tourist with him again on Saturday, she didn't have the heart to refuse. He grumbled because the Statue of Liberty was closed for renovation, but had more fun than she did shopping at Macy's, Gimbels, and Orbach's, selecting gifts for a host of relatives, including his mother, then insisting that Kate let him buy her a little parting present.

"This," he said, pointing to an oversize red canvas shoulder bag in one of Macy's specialty departments. "I want to be sure you never dump that old purse of yours in front of another guy."

"You make it sound deliberate!"

"I'd be flattered if it had been."

"You really shouldn't buy me anything."

"I'm going to anyway. It's up to you whether you help me pick it out."

"All right," she agreed reluctantly, "but I haven't a thing to wear with that shade of red. Do you like this cream-colored one?"

She fingered a bag that cost half of what the red one did, worried that his big splurge in New York was costing more than he could afford.

"If you like it, I do." He paid with a credit card, a pleased grin on his face.

She wasn't home Saturday night to know if Alex called. After convincing Bill that another gourmet meal would make the waistbands of her skirts uncomfortably snug, she really enjoyed a hot dog from a pushcart, then walked hand in hand with the big, comfortable man until they had to rush to make a nine-o'clock movie. They parted on her stoop after sharing a long, sweet, undemanding kiss.

Awaking with the cramps that heralded the beginning of her period, Kate slid down to the end of the hide-a-bed and searched for her slippers, too sleepy to get up and too melancholy to stay in bed thinking. Later she would join Bill for a final afternoon together, then bring him back to her apartment for an early supper. He had to leave for the airport before six thirty.

Hoping it was only her time of month that made her feel so depressed, she glanced at the desk calendar sitting near the phone. Memorial Day weekend, she noted with little interest, not especially wanting the extra day off on Monday. Bill would fly into Des Moines later tonight, pick up his car,

112

then visit his mother for a day before returning to work on Tuesday. Kate couldn't begrudge the widow a day with her son, but New York was going to be awfully lonesome when Bill was gone. She had come to think of him as her best friend. Worse, he was her only defense against her turbulent feelings for Alex.

Roughly yanking on the sheets and pounding the pillows, she made her bed and flipped the mattress back into place, haphazardly tossing the cushions into place. The metal bar under the mattress gave her a kink in her back, and sleeping in a living room was the pits. This morning it was hard to remember why she'd been so eager to come to New York. Her last apartment had been spacious compared with this. Only four blocks from the museum, it had three high-ceilinged rooms and a nice back porch for sunbathing.

Trying to blame her grumpiness on her period didn't work. Her reasons for wanting Bill to stay were so selfish, she didn't much like herself. The prospect of seeing Alex at work day after day without the big man's friendship behind her was unnerving.

An hour later she was casually dressed in a white wraparound skirt and a navy top when the phone rang. Any other time she would have been delighted to hear her father's voice on the other end, but he was much too sensitive to her moods. The most charitable thing to call her disposition today was foul.

"Sweetheart," her father boomed, "how's the big city treating you?"

"Great, Dad. I sold a highboy last week. You won't believe what a decorator paid for it."

"Good going. Your mother is standing here telling me what to say. Are you having any fun?"

"When I have time. I've seen a lot of the tourist spots— the Empire State Building, Greenwich Village, places like that."

113

"Your mother wants to know if you're meeting any nice people."

Her great-great aunt wasn't the only one worried about her single status.

"I've been to several parties with Mr. Gilbert, making business contacts. And the women at work are very nice." She heard him repeat this to her mother.

"Mom wants to talk," he said with a chuckle. "Is there anything you need, Katie?"

An armor-plated heart, she thought wryly, so Alex's no-love policy wouldn't hurt quite so much.

"Just your love and support, Dad."

"You always have that. We're proud of what you're doing, sweetheart."

He hadn't been fooled in the least. If the summer selling season wasn't in full swing, he would probably hop on a plane and come to New York to check on her. She didn't need that!

"How long are the skirts there?" her mother asked, always curious about the latest fashions.

"A variety of lengths. Almost anything goes."

That wasn't what she wanted to hear; her mother liked definite guidelines in everything. She might forgive a love affair with one man, but she would never understand how her daughter could make love with Alex and still want to spend time with Bill. Kate didn't understand it herself.

Her parents' call hadn't done a thing to cheer her. She took two pills for her cramps and started putting together a chicken salad from the chunks she had diced the day before. A casual supper with toasted English muffins would have to see Bill on his way. Maybe he would eat again on the plane.

They went to the United Nations, enjoying a tour hosted by a striking young woman from India, even though no meetings were in session that Sunday afternoon. Kate enjoyed the art contributed by member nations and the gift shops in the basement. While Bill wrote a stack of postcards to be mailed to his uncle, a stamp collector, from the UN post office, she bought him a souvenir pen. It wasn't a romantic gift, but she could see him holding the substantial writing instrument in his big, powerful hand. He seemed extremely pleased with it.

"I've been trying to decide for days how to do this," he said as they walked hand in hand down Forty-fifth Street just to enjoy the warmth of the sun and each other's company. "I didn't come up with any clever plan, so I'll have to ask you straight out." He stopped and took both her hands in his. "Kate, marry me."

She wasn't totally surprised, but she was at a loss for an answer.

"I know Iowa isn't as exciting as New York," he went on, "but we could have a good life together. Kids, a nice home. I travel a lot now, but most of the time you can come with me until we have a family for you to look after. I wouldn't expect you to give up the antiques business until then. I guess I'm saying everything but the most important thing. Kate, I love you."

"I care a lot about you, Bill." She freed her hands and started slowly walking again.

"Care isn't a very strong emotion." He sounded sad, not angry.

"Right now it's the best I can do. I really like you, Bill. More than like."

"Is it your job?"

"No, I'm not at all sure I belong here. Probably I don't. I was so eager to deal in fine antiques, but . . ." She couldn't explain the hollow feeling inside her, and he wouldn't understand the hold Alex had on her emotions. "We haven't known each other very long."

Putting his arm around her waist, he held her close to his side as they walked, oblivious to passing pedestrians and traffic.

"You haven't said no?" he asked, looking for the positive side of the situation, as he always did.

"No." Her voice was a hoarse whisper. How easy it would be to say yes and return to the kind of life she had left behind.

"I won't give up easily." He smiled down at her with an expression that would have brought tears to her eyes if she hadn't been studying the sidewalk with the intensity of a child hunting for lost pennies.

"I hate to see you leave." This she could say with total honesty.

"I hate to leave you here. New York is a nice place to visit, but I wouldn't want to live here."

Kate smiled, wondering how many thousands of tourists said that same thing every day.

Disappointment didn't dull Bill's appetite. Back at her apartment he finished four buttered muffin halves with half of the large bowl of chicken salad, while she only picked at her food. Her cramps had gone, but she still felt logy and dejected.

The buzzer sounded, but she didn't jump to respond.

"I'll answer, honey," Bill offered, then boomed a loud "Who's there?" down to the unexpected visitor.

"Alex Gilbert. Is Kate there?"

"Your boss?" Bill whispered to her, inviting Alex to come up when she nodded an affirmative answer, too slow-thinking to come up with an excuse to send him away. From past experience she didn't suppose he would leave anyway.

The two men shook hands at the door, exchanging pleasantries as though they belonged to different branches of the same lodge. She didn't want them to punch each other, but they didn't have to sound so darned cordial!

"What brings you to New York?" Alex asked, lowering himself onto her platform rocker, looking like he belonged at an exclusive yacht club in his white linen slacks and a knit top with a little polo player on the pocket.

"I'm in the meat business. Sales," Bill offered. "Would you like some chicken salad? Kate toasted a few too many muffins here too."

Why was he playing host in her home? To her dismay, Alex accepted, moving gracefully to the small Formica table that served her for everything from dining to bill paying.

"How long will you be here?" Alex asked after exchanging a few comments about the weather with both of them.

"Another twenty minutes," Bill admitted. "I have a plane to catch."

"Too bad." Alex bit into one of the muffins left on the platter. "I'd like to hear more about the meat business. Nothing I like better than a good steak."

"Bill sells a lot of liver and pork too," Kate said. "The best restaurants and hotel chains buy from him."

"Is liver a big specialty?" Alex asked, picking a black olive from the chicken salad before taking a bite.

"With the orders I've gotten on this trip, we'll be running liver-packing shifts around the clock."

Kate escaped to the bathroom, the only sanctuary in the tiny apartment, and splashed handful after handful of cold water on her face. What was Alex doing here? Why did he think he could drop in unannounced anytime the mood hit him? If he cared about her at all, why had he waited more than a week to show some sign of it? She went back into the room with damp hair edging her forehead.

"Sorry we didn't meet sooner," Bill was saying, standing beside the big nylon-sided suitcase and briefcase that he had left at the apartment to save time when he went to the airport.

Kate didn't have to be a mind reader to guess what Alex was thinking. When she offered to see Bill down to his cab, Alex assured her he would be there finishing his coffee. He stood to shake hands with the other man, and it might have passed as a friendly grip if she hadn't seen the white knuckles on her employer's hand.

"Well, nice meeting you." Alex hadn't sounded that insincere talking to Myra Webster!

When she and Bill stopped in the lobby, a good-bye kiss was the last thing on Kate's mind.

"Why did you invite him up?"

"He is your boss." Bill sounded a little sullen.

"You could've said I wasn't home."

"Why? He's only the guy you work for, isn't he? Or is he the big attraction in this city?"

"Of course not! He's my employer. That's all!"

"Then why are you so uptight?"

"Did you ever consider that I may not want you to leave?" she asked miserably.

"I'm not saying good-bye for long," he promised. "I'm not going to give up. I want to get you away from this town. This is no place for a sweet kid from Nebraska."

"I'm not a kid," she said, torn between basking in his concern and resenting his patronizing tone.

"I know that, baby." He glanced out at the prompt taxi and kissed her soundly. "You'll be hearing from me."

"Have a safe flight," she called after him.

Slowly, as though each foot were weighed down with a lead boot, she climbed the three flights to the room where Alex was waiting. He was standing at the window with his back to her, hands in his pants pockets and his shoulders hunched.

"These curtains are falling apart," he said grimly.

So was she.

"They come with the apartment."

"I didn't know he was living here."

"He wasn't!"

"He just happened to drop by with a suitcase?"

"It was easier to check out of his hotel at noon and leave his luggage here while we went to the UN."

"Sure."

"It's none of your business anyway!"

118

"No?" He turned slowly, fixing his eyes on her face with an intensity that might have made her cringe if she hadn't been so angry.

"I didn't hear from you all week!"

"You would've, if you'd spent any time at all in your own apartment," he said angrily.

"I was here every night—alone!"

"I go to bed before midnight. I can't wait up until dawn for you to get home when I'm working sixteen hours a day."

"If you're so hardworking, why do you avoid the gallery?"

"That's a childish question. You know buying is the crux of the business. I can hire people to mind the store."

"I realize that. I'm one of the hired hands."

"You're more than that!" He took two steps closer, thrusting his hands even deeper into his pockets, pulling the finely woven linen taut over his thighs.

"Then why are you being so disagreeable?" she demanded.

"Disagreeable! I'm frigging furious! I make love to a woman, and she spends the next week with some clown from Iowa!"

"He's not a clown! He's a kind, considerate, pleasant man. You could take some lessons from him in good manners!"

"Good manners!"

"And don't mimic me!"

"I'm not!" He moved to within inches of her. "What I want to know is why!"

"Why what?"

"Why him?"

"He's friendly and kind. I have a right to see anyone I like. I do my work, and at night this apartment seems pretty . . ." She paused for a long moment. "Empty."

"You were going to say lonely." It was an accusation.

"Quiet," she insisted.

"I have to go to Amsterdam. Will you come with me?"

His habit of suddenly switching topics would drive her crazy!

"On business?"

"No, I don't need your help with the buying. It would be better for my business to leave you in charge here."

"What about your policy of keeping business and pleasure separate?"

"You can't possibly be as naive as you act sometimes!" He went to her then, trapping her shoulders in a hard grip.

"I am not naive!" She tried to free herself but refused to compromise her dignity by struggling.

"You are if you expect me to believe the meat packer is just a platonic buddy."

"He *is* just a good friend!"

"Is that what you want from a man, friendship?"

He kissed her then, but she didn't like it. His forcefulness only made her go rigid in his arms.

"I'm not good at sharing," he said harshly.

"And I'm not one of your toys," she hissed.

He ran his hands over her upper arms, as though warming her skin could thaw her heart.

"I'm not trying to treat you like one," he said in a softer voice, walking to the couch and sitting on the edge, his eyes downcast. "Jealous rages aren't my usual style," he added.

"You could've fooled me." When she was really angry, she didn't let go of it so quickly.

"All right, I'm sorry," he grumbled.

"You say it, but you don't mean it."

"Of course I don't mean it!" He stood again and restlessly paced in and out of the kitchen alcove. "But why him?"

He can't look that miserable and not care at all, Kate thought, catching her breath as she watched him find a glass and get a drink of water.

"You probably drank the rest of my Bordeaux with him," he said bitterly.

She couldn't deny that, so she ignored it.

"In many ways Bill is my kind of person," she said, trying to explain. "He grew up in a small midwestern town like I did. We have a lot in common."

"How much time can you spend talking about good old times with someone you picked up at the Met?"

"I didn't pick him up, not the way you mean it, and I have fun with Bill."

"What kind of fun?" he asked suspiciously.

"Just plain old fun—sight-seeing, walking in the park, doing ordinary things. You're so jaded by all those parties you go to, you don't know how to have fun."

"Is that really what you think?" He edged closer, the glint in his eyes making her wary.

"Yes," she murmured softly.

"Is this fun, Katie?"

He took her into his arms, kissing her slowly, holding her against him while he gently drew her lips between his.

"No!" She surprised herself by vigorously pushing him away.

"That isn't fun for you?" He sounded genuinely hurt.

"Oh, it is," she admitted reluctantly, "but there's more to liking someone. It's sharing little things—a walk in the park, an organ grinder, a parade."

"Then we haven't had any real fun together?" He seemed more weary than hurt.

"I know you're my employer, and I know you can be wonderful, but I don't really *know* you."

"He really didn't stay here this week?"

"No. There's only been you."

She hated herself for giving him this reassurance. Did she ask him if his wealthy clients tempted him with anything besides their money? Did she pry into his life before they met? Never, even in her wishful thinking, did she imagine he hadn't made love to other women. Only the glimmer of happiness on his face salvaged her pride.

121

"Katie." The soft, liquid tone in his voice sounded alarm warnings for her. "Come here."

"No, I don't think so, Alex."

"Have you put last Saturday out of your mind?"

"No." She never would. "I've been worried about the sofa leg."

His laugh was halfhearted. "It can be fixed."

"But you'll lose a lot on a repaired piece."

"Stop it, Kate!"

"What?"

"Antiques. Whenever you're insecure, you switch the conversation to business."

"I do not! You pay me a good salary to keep my mind on the gallery."

"Wrong! I pay you to help me make more money. That doesn't make our relationship one long business meeting."

"We don't have a relationship! You promised we'd have a professional association."

"I wondered when you would mention that." He moistened his lips with the tip of his tongue and walked back to the window.

"I'm sorry."

He gazed in her direction, but this time he didn't tell her not to apologize.

"I wanted what happened as much as you did. I'm not blaming you," she admitted.

Regarding her in silent speculation, he made her feel like a specimen under study.

"I don't suppose there's any chance you're on the pill?"

"No."

"If you were pregnant, you'd tell me? You wouldn't try to make other arrangements?"

"As of this morning I'm absolutely certain I'm not. What do you mean by other arrangements?" She would never, never want to get rid of a child. Did he think she would?

"Marry someone else just because he's better father material." He wandered back to the kitchen alcove, seemingly unable to stay in one spot.

"That does it!" Her temper snapped, and she grabbed for the nearest object, a throw pillow on the couch, and hurled it toward him, missing her target but smashing the glass he'd used for water. It shattered in a hundred pieces on the counter, some of which fell to the carpeted floor. "Just go! Just leave me alone!"

He did the worst possible thing: he laughed and then started brushing the glass fragments into a pile, using a sheet of paper toweling.

"I can do that myself!"

"Darling . . ." He came to her.

She didn't intend to kiss him; she didn't want to cling to him with dry sobs shaking her body. It wasn't fair that he had magical hands that soothed away her anger and made her want to melt against him.

"You taste so wonderful," he said, slowly blessing every inch of her face with gentle, sensual kisses.

"I don't belong here," she said more to herself than to him.

"In my arms?" He flicked a honey-streaked lock from her forehead and brushed the spot with his lips.

"No, in this city. In your business. With your clients."

"Have Myra and her cohorts intimidated you that much?"

"Not exactly. No." How could she possibly explain her feeling of displacement? Would she ever know where she stood in his life?

"Do you know what tomorrow is?"

She stared at him blankly, unable to dredge up any special significance for the day.

"Memorial Day. School's out. Shop's closed. Our day off."

"I thought I'd go to the gallery anyway and work on—"

"No way! As your employer I order you not to work there alone after hours. Too many things can happen."

They already had.

"Tomorrow," he went on, "I'll be here at eight o'clock. That's A.M., morning. Dress casually."

"Did you ever think of asking instead of telling me?"

"Katie, will you play with me tomorrow?"

"Play!"

"You want fun, we'll have fun. I guarantee it."

"Doing what?"

"You'll find out."

He smacked her lips noisily, affectionately squeezed her bottom, then left without giving her time to refuse his invitation, if that was what it was.

It took her a few seconds to realize she had a bona fide date with Alex.

CHAPTER SEVEN

Alex arrived early, but Kate was ready, dressed in white designer jeans, an aquamarine sleeveless top that brought out the blue in her eyes, and comfortable sandals. She expected to spend the day rummaging through flea markets; antiques dealers were notorious for combining business and pleasure, and Alex was sure to have discovered some activity. Memorial Day weekend heralded the beginning of the outdoor season, and she loved a big country sale with everything from straw hats to old tractors being hawked by amateurs and pros. In actual practice, flea markets were often conglomerations of disreputable junk haphazardly displayed and outrageously overpriced, but the possibility of finding a real gem gave them the allure of a treasure hunt. Kate approached even the least promising with memories of past finds: a box of bright-colored Fiesta dinnerware for five dollars, a necklace with ivory beads for two, a balloon-back chair in need of refinishing for eight. Her emergency cash, usually kept in a saltbox in the kitchen cupboard, was tucked in her purse just in case.

"You look nice," Alex said when she opened the door for him.

She was about to tell him that the jeans were starting their third season, but his expression stopped her. Maybe too much honesty was just as bad as unnecessary apologies.

"Thank you," she said, smiling sweetly. "So do you."

He did know how to dress. His beltless beige slacks

125

molded his hips and had just the right amount of fullness in the legs, and his chocolate-brown knit shirt had an alligator on the pocket. "You won't need a jacket," he said, watching her take a yellow nylon windbreaker from the closet.

"Just superstition," she said self-consciously. "Carry an umbrella and you'll never need to use it."

He laughed indulgently.

Their early start didn't save them from congested highways. By the time Alex reached the New Jersey Turnpike, traffic had become more than moderately heavy.

"Everyone's going somewhere today," she commented.

"Coming back will be much worse, bumper to bumper."

"Are we going far?" Why was she so hesitant about asking what he had planned for the day?

"Hocking Hill."

"Hocking Hill." She tested the sound of the name. "I've never heard of it."

"Never heard of Hocking Hill's Memorial Day Muster?" He tut-tutted. "Only place in New Jersey where a fife-and-drum corps leads a rodeo parade."

"You're putting me on."

"No, we're going to have fun today." He couldn't have announced a six-week stint at a Marine Corps boot camp any more grimly.

Hocking Hill was a tree-shaded community, proud of its eighteenth-century houses. A business district stretched along the main street for several blocks. Though it looked like a sedate bedroom community, Alex assured her the town was the toothpaste capital of New Jersey. Judging by the congestion on the street and the overflow of pedestrian traffic on the narrow sidewalks, there were ten visitors for every resident present for the festivities.

"Parade will start in about an hour," Alex said, putting his station wagon under the watchful care of some teenagers in a church lot and paying their fee for parking. "Then this

126

afternoon there's the big cowboy rodeo, and of course, we'll do the carnival before the day's over."

"No flea market? No auction?"

"Not that I know of. Are you disappointed?"

"No, just surprised. You have absolutely no ulterior motive for coming here?"

"Of course I do, but not a business reason. I want to spend the day with you." He squeezed her hand and pulled her along in the stream of people moving toward the main street.

The police were manning wooden barriers, diverting cars from the business blocks in preparation for the parade. The bleachers flanking the street for several blocks were already nearly full with spectators. Alex saw a man in a straw hat and a carpenter's apron taking tickets from people before they climbed the planks; the seats, the man informed him, had been sold out weeks ago.

"Hope you don't mind standing," Alex said, tucking Kate's hand in the crook of his arm.

"Not at all. I love parades! This is marvelous, Alex. Where did you hear about it?"

"I asked a neighbor what simple folk do on Memorial Day," he said with a trace of sarcasm, the first indication that he was still annoyed about finding Bill in her apartment.

"There's nothing simple about you." He was the most complicated man she'd ever met.

"Do you really know me that well, Katie?" He softened the challenge with a smile.

"Do you want me to know you well?"

"That depends." His face was guarded and his comment ambiguous. "Did you have breakfast?"

"No." She'd been too excited about spending the day with him.

"Let's see what we can find."

The café on Main Street was closed for the day, but a small flagstone rest area—a minipark created by the city

127

when an old building was demolished—was lined on either side with food stands set up by local civic organizations. They found one selling homemade nut buns and steaming coffee and made a meal of the sticky yeast rolls. She laughed when a sliver of nut stuck to his chin, and he got even by stealing the last of her bun.

"Your sweet tooth is going to give you a little round pot," she warned.

"And if you keep sampling all those weird gourmet concoctions, you're going to end up with—"

"Never mind!"

"I was going to say chronic indigestion."

"I'll bet!"

They wandered about holding hands. A policeman directed them to the fairgrounds where the rodeo and carnival were set up. In a side street the high-school marching band was warming up with discordant bursts of sound while farther away men and women in cowboy gear kept a tight rein on their well-trained horses as they waited for the parade to begin. Entertained by the bustle of preparations, Kate and Alex walked to the end of the units being assembled, then crossed the street to return to the main route. Kate picked her way carefully across the roadway, only too aware that the horses had passed that way. Alex didn't and, as a result, spent several minutes irritably working his soiled Italian loafer back and forth on the lawn of a house with a For Sale sign and boarded windows. When he suggested they return to a more civilized street, his smile was a crooked grimace.

The mayor led the parade in a convertible escorted by motorcycle policemen whose helmets with wind guards gave them a formidable macho appearance. Alex had found a viewing spot behind a family comfortably seated in lawn chairs, the mother ignoring a tot in a stroller who seemed determined to retrieve a fallen bottle of milk or land on his head trying. An older boy was waving a great wad of cotton candy like a baton, occasionally gobbling a bite that turned

128

his mouth pink and sticky, but mostly content to threaten bystanders with the sugary fluff. Alex was his first victim, catching a big glob on the front of his slacks when the boy started arguing with a pigtailed little girl who had to be his sibling.

"Would you mind watching it, son?" Alex asked with admirable control, rewarded by a look of sheer malevolence from the mother.

He brushed the candied mess ineffectively with a clean handkerchief, succeeding only in spreading the grainy pink splotches.

"Sugar washes out," Kate assured him, holding back a chuckle.

Alex took her arm and guided her farther along the street, finally finding a wedge in the crowd where they both could see the drum-and-fife corps passing by in their military costumes patterned after Revolutionary War uniforms. Kate found their performance stirring, but Alex scowled until he noticed that she was watching him, not the parade.

"Outstanding group," he said.

"Very colorful," she agreed, feeling like tapping her toe to the measured beat of the drums.

Every local man who'd ever served in the military marched behind the drum-and-fife corps, with a single revered survivor of World War I passing on a special float draped in red, white, and blue bunting. Veterans of World War II looked soldierly and proud in spite of their age and far outnumbered the younger men from the Korean and Vietnam wars. Kate reached for Alex's hand, squeezing tightly and sharing the grim look on his face; their generation had been a fortunate one, not called upon for the life-shattering sacrifice of war. She prayed hard that those younger than they would be spared too.

Auxiliary followed auxiliary—mothers, wives, maybe even sisters and grandmothers following the veterans; then came the baton twirlers, local clowns, and a host of boys on bicycles decorated with red, white, and blue crepe paper. Boy Scouts, Sea Scouts, Girl Scouts, and Cubs followed with their leaders, blasted along by a junior-high band that played with more enthusiasm than finesse. Alex guided her down the street to another viewing spot, although they couldn't see as well from the new location.

The high-school band preceded a motorcycle demonstration by the sheriff's department that was loudly cheered, the noisy maneuvers timed to the second to avoid collisions. By the time the equestrian section of the parade brought up the rear, Alex's face had set in a mask of boredom. He walked back to the car with his eyes on the ground.

"It was a nice parade," Kate ventured.

"Yes." He seemed a little startled. "It's commendable when the whole town turns out like that."

The two-mile drive from the church parking lot to the fairgrounds took just under an hour, with Alex fuming because his motor seemed to be heating up too much at the slow stop-and-go pace.

"We could go home," Kate suggested.

"And miss all the fun? Not a chance." He flashed her a very good imitation of a smile.

"Are you doing this to prove something?" she asked suspiciously.

"Aren't you enjoying it?"

"The parade was fun, but I don't want you to be miserable."

"I'm not," he denied sharply, then silently concentrated on inching through the mass of cars and pedestrians headed for the afternoon activities.

They bought breaded hot dogs on sticks, but Alex threw his away after one bite—he thought it looked greenish—and ate instead a huge container of caramel corn with peanuts. Kate would have loved some cotton candy on a rolled paper stick but decided not to ask him to stand in line for one. He seemed to have forgotten his pink-speckled slacks, and she preferred not to remind him.

"I love rides!" she said as they made their way down the midway.

"I'll try to win you a stuffed bear," Alex suggested, eyeing a baseball booth with obvious misgivings.

"I don't have room for a stuffed ant in my apartment," she said, tugging on his arm. "Look, whirling teacups. Let's try that." She pulled him toward a line in front of a red wooden ticket booth with a leering mad hare painted above the grillwork opening.

"I love roller coasters," she said, caught up in the excitement of the carnival. "Too bad there's none here."

"Too bad. Don't you think this line is too long to stand in?"

"No, they're giving skimpy, short rides. We'll be on it in a few minutes."

They were, wiggling down onto low wooden seats and clasping the metal bar that an attendant locked across their stomachs. Kate cried out with delight when the wild, tilting ride began, loving it when the little wooden cup was flung furiously in one direction, then jerked back in another, twirling and whirling while the platform went through frantic upheavals, time after time threatening to capsize the cup or ram into another one. She bounded up breathless and laughing when their turn was over.

"That was too short," she said.

Alex didn't say anything. She followed him away from the ride, uneasy now about his silent retreat.

"Are you all right?" she asked.

"Great."

He hurried toward a rest area, the green wooden slatted benches occupied mostly by elderly people and women with young babies. Spotting a space beside a corpulent, white-haired woman who was fanning herself with a piece of newspaper, he sank down, letting his head drop between his knees.

Alarmed now, Kate hovered over him, genuinely worried when she touched his forehead and found it cold and clammy. He looked up impatiently, his complexion an unhealthy grayish-green.

"Why didn't you tell me you get sick on rides?" She didn't know whether to feel angry or guilty.

"I haven't been on one in twenty years!"

"You picked a fine time to try one, then."

"We're supposed to be having *fun!*" The word, as he said it, suggested some kind of lunacy.

"I'm not having fun if you're not! Are you going to be okay?"

"I'm fine. Come on." He grabbed her hand and pulled her toward the grandstand, insisting they get tickets for the rodeo, although the last ones available only allowed them to sit on the grassy slope at one end of the outdoor arena.

"Wouldn't you rather go home?" Kate asked anxiously.

"No, we're going to the rodeo." He sounded tense enough to throttle her.

From their spot on the grass, with the chain-link fencing behind them, they had a fairly good view of the activity below. Alex rested his arms on his knees, not looking in her direction. His skin had lost its greenish tinge, but he still looked pallid.

"I haven't seen a rodeo in years," she said, testing his reaction before letting him see her enthusiasm.

"Craziest sport in the country," he said sourly. "We had to wear helmets to knock a puck around on ice. These rodeo riders get bounced on their heads with nothing but a little piece of felt between their skulls and five hundred pounds of horses' hooves."

"A lot of men seem to find it exciting," she reminded him. Really, Alex was anything but fun today!

"I'm blowing this," he said glumly.

"Yeah, you are. But why insist we come here when you don't enjoy any of it?"

"I wanted you to have a good time," he explained.

"How can I do that when you're miserable?"

"I didn't plan to be miserable!"

"The drive was tedious, you're not wild about parades, rides nauseate you, and cowboys leave you cold. What did you expect to enjoy here?" she insisted.

"You."

"Oh."

"Come here." He held out his arm, cradling her shoulders when she moved closer.

"You're sick. We should go."

"I'm feeling better. I wanted to do something with you besides dragging you to parties you don't like."

"Well, they're business."

"Not entirely. I enjoy them."

"People were very nice to me at the last one," she admitted. "Most of them."

"Who wasn't nice?"

"Oh, never mind." She wasn't going to tell him the host got fresh.

The public-address system was more than effective, and a drawling voice boomed out over the crowd, signaling the beginning of the rodeo. Alex lay back on the grass, muttering about grass stains and not pretending any interest, but Kate watched avidly, enjoying the acrobatic antics of the clown as he did his life-saving distractions, allowing fallen riders to leave the arena safely. She wouldn't want to be in love with one of the cowboys; she, too, thought their profession was too hazardous, much as she hated to agree with Alex. Their women must live in dread of every event. Being thrown off angry livestock was a heck of a way to make a living.

Incredibly, Alex seemed to doze, oblivious to the roar of the crowd below them and the cheers of the other spectators

133

dotting the slope. She watched the whole show before rousing him.

"Did you enjoy the rodeo?" she teased.

"Immensely. I may even be able to eat again." He yawned and rose lazily to his feet, pulling her up with him.

Making their way back to the car, they stopped only to buy a silly bird mounted on a willowy stick, which made a wheezing sound.

"You hated today," she said.

"Most of it," he admitted. "Not being with you. What are you going to do with the ridiculous bird?" He eyed the vivid yellow creature with bright pink feathers, wrinkling his nose in disdain.

"Hang it on your Art Deco group to remind us both of today."

"Not in my office, you're not!" He sounded firm, but smiled.

"We're too different, Alex." The truth made her miserable.

"Because I get sick on silly rides?" He was edging the station wagon out of the crowded fairgrounds parking area.

"No, you know it's not that."

"We have a lot to talk about." He honked at a trio of adolescent boys who were chasing each other, ducking in front of moving cars, oblivious to the danger of being hit. "As soon as I get out of this damn traffic!"

They stopped at a lovely inn with white siding and long green shutters, only to learn that there would be a two-hour wait for a table. Neither felt up to two hours of drinking in the lounge, so they left without eating.

Traffic was bumper to bumper on the New Jersey Turnpike, creating the worst possible conditions for any kind of conversation. Except for an occasional outburst from Alex about the insane driving habits of the average motorist, the last hour passed in silence. Kate couldn't remember ever having spent such a bad day with anyone. It wouldn't have mattered if she wasn't in love with him.

Leaning back on the headrest and pretending to shut out the congestion of the road, she studied the man beside her through the fuzziness of her lowered lashes. If his face was too flawed to be conventionally handsome, it was beautiful to her; the brow was broken by one long crease when he frowned, as he was doing now. Maybe she loved his cheekbones best—those high, smooth prominences above the beginnings of a shadowy beard. Or was it his strong chin that was so special? She was dying to trace its lean hard line with her fingers. She couldn't think about his mouth without yearning to feel it on hers, and his eyes under heavy lashes had the power to reduce her to a mass of raw emotions.

She sighed, rewarded by a brief touch of his hand on her thigh.

"I thought you were sleeping," he said softly.

"No, just thinking."

"About what?"

"I don't want to tell you."

"That's encouraging."

The long daylight of late spring lasted until he reached her neighborhood. He drove down a street devoid of parking spaces and finally found a spot some ten blocks from her apartment.

"Did you have a terrible time today?" he asked solemnly, unbuckling his seat belt and facing her.

"No, I like being with you. I'm only sorry you hated it all."

"Katie, I could never hate being anywhere with you."

He leaned over and kissed her, at first gently, then more forcefully, catching his breath with pleasure when he drew away.

"This isn't where I live, you know," she whispered.

"I've been thinking what to say to you all the way home," he admitted ruefully.

"What did you decide on?"

"The truth, only I'm not sure what it is."

"What truth?"

His hand found hers, lacing their fingers together on the seat between them.

"I've wanted you since you walked into my office for your interview," he admitted without meeting her eyes.

"Is that why you hired me?"

If he said yes, she couldn't possibly go back to the gallery.

"Absolutely not! Your credentials were so good, I decided to talk to you before making any other appointments for interviews. No others were necessary."

"I can't work for you if you don't think I'm capable."

"You're more than capable. I'm very fortunate to have you working for me."

"Thank you."

"I was upset about that joker from Iowa answering your phone when we talked about Purvis. That's the only reason I was critical."

"Don't call Bill a joker or a clown or any other derogatory name. He's a good friend of mine."

"Would you rather I punch him in the nose?"

"Of course not! He might hurt you!"

"Thanks a lot. You can't expect me to like him."

"There's no reason why you should. Just don't put him down."

"I'm sorry. You're right, of course." He seemed truly contrite. "Jealousy isn't usually my style."

"It doesn't look good on you."

"Sometimes I really like you," he said unexpectedly.

"Only sometimes?" She felt a little hurt.

"Do you know what it's like, caring for someone and not wanting the responsibilities that go with caring?"

"I know that sometimes people care—and life would be much simpler if they didn't."

"Let's stop talking about 'people' when it's you and me we mean."

"All right."

"I thought of driving straight to my apartment."

"I'm glad you didn't." She looked at him, but his face was in the shadow, as the sun had disappeared behind a bulky brick building. Her eyes had a terrible habit of tearing at the worst times.

"You won't be if I tell you why I stopped here instead."

She didn't say anything.

"I can't share you with—what's-his-name."

"Bill."

"But I'm not ready to offer you enough to make you exclusively mine. Kate, I feel like I'm caught in a vise."

She felt the same way. Her life would be so simple, so secure, if she could say yes to Bill and go back to the Midwest with him. She wasn't tough enough or shrewd enough to be a New York dealer. Worse, she didn't know how to fight for what she wanted from Alex.

"I want you with me, but I don't want to be responsible for your happiness. I don't want to hurt you, Kate."

It wasn't enough to say she understood. Touching his cheek with her fingers, she wondered why love had to have this painful, turbulent side. His eyes begged her to say she didn't need commitments, strings, promises. Knowing that a word, a sign, from her would lead to wonderful days and nights of love, she also knew they were impossible on his terms. Hot tears escaped from the corners of her eyes as Alex moved close, catching one on his tongue, kissing away another.

Bill had offered her what her heart secretly yearned for: one man to love her wholly and completely for all time. She never doubted his capacity to do this; he would let his passion ripen into lifelong faithfulness and love. The man beside her now could offer only release from the sexual tensions that made their time together a torment. How terrible that she loved Alex too much to come to him for simple pleasure; how awful that she didn't love Bill when her welfare so clearly lay with him.

"It wasn't the parade or the carnival," he said. "I'd wallow naked in a tub of cotton candy or swing upside down on the Ferris wheel if it would bring you to me."

She had to smile at these ridiculous images, but the truth behind them wasn't funny. The day had been an utter failure, not because Alex hated the entertainment but because their needs and wants were worlds apart. The tension was like a glass wall separating them; they just didn't belong in the same world. He could never be a loving, dependable husband and father; she could never be happy having a sophisticated, uncommitted affair. What was necessary for her was an unthinkable burden for him.

His tender kiss only added to her pain. She pulled away, telling him without words that what he wanted was impossible.

Without a word he drove back to her apartment, then watched as she gathered her purse and the jacket she hadn't needed, deliberately leaving the silly bird on the backseat.

"Thank you, Alex." She was completing a ritual, not thanking him for the day.

"I'm going to Candlebrook, then to Amsterdam. I probably won't see you before I leave."

"Have a nice trip, then."

"You're in charge at the gallery until I get back. I'm not sure when that will be. I will need some vacation after my buying in the Netherlands is done."

"Yes, I'm sure you work too hard."

"Damn it, Katie!" He seemed about to say more but instead clamped his lips tightly together.

"Have a nice trip, Alex." She didn't even realize she was repeating herself.

"Take care," he said dryly, driving away the moment she was safely inside the outer door.

CHAPTER EIGHT

The week passed with grating slowness, even though Kate managed to keep furiously busy at work, arriving long before Jack Fisher every morning and leaving in the evening only because both Blanche and Nancy insisted she not stay there alone after closing time. Alex stayed in Connecticut until departing for the Netherlands on Thursday, leaving a message with Blanche that concerned only a few business arrangements.

Sunday afternoon Bill called. He painted a glowing word picture of his activities of that week but failed to coax her into joining him in Iowa. Her already low spirits drooped even further. Cozy housekeeping with a man she didn't love was no substitute for what she needed from Alex. At first evasive and then downright discouraging, she tried to let Bill know there was no hope for them, but his obstinate optimism couldn't be shaken by anything she said on the phone.

"You'll change your mind, sweetheart," he promised. "I've got another week's vacation coming, and as soon as I can get away, we'll talk all this out."

She was afraid to have him come to New York again. In her present mood she might be tempted to grasp at straws and accept his offer of escape.

After Bill's call she threw herself into her work even more frantically, contacting old clients with the zeal of a missionary and making several sales through sheer persuasiveness. By Thursday she was physically exhausted, her eyes bleary from late nights of poring over the files she had carried home to study.

Buoyed up by a successful appointment—she'd just contracted to buy a Belter parlor set, a fine example of the most elaborate style of Victorian furniture—she dashed up the stairs to the second-floor office to find Myra Webster trying her best to intimidate Blanche.

Kate stood for a moment, unseen by Alex's important client. Myra wore a jersey sheath in a moss-green shade that was bad for her complexion, flushed now after a heated debate with the secretary. Kate felt a sudden rush of pity for the socialite. No one could go through three husbands without emotional scars, and it was more pathetic than threatening that she needed to pursue a man as young as Alex, purchasing antiques she might not even want as a wedge to get his attention.

"Can I help you, Mrs. Webster?" she asked, letting sympathy show in her face and voice.

"Oh, Miss . . ."

"Bevan. Kate Bevan."

"You can tell me when Alex will be back. This secretary makes it sound like he's on a secret spy mission or something. I need something special for my niece's wedding."

"I'm afraid his plans were unsure when he left. What kind of gift did you have in mind?"

"Oh, I'll wait for Alex," she said impatiently. "He can't hide out in the Netherlands forever."

This time the woman's snappy rejection only challenged Kate. "We do have something special for brides, but it may be gone before he returns."

With expert coaxing, Kate led Myra down to the salesroom, where she showed her the lovely pink bride's basket, stressing how sentimental and scarce the fine glass piece was. Still grumbling about Alex's absence, Myra not only bought the basket but thanked Kate for pointing it out.

"I've always been fond of my niece," she said with none of her usual arrogance.

"Alex will be pleased the bride's basket is going to someone special," Kate said as a parting gift to her new client.

The sale to Myra cheered her as nothing had since the Hocking Hill Memorial Day Muster. She could more than handle the business in Alex's absence. Matching antiques and potential owners was an art, and she'd guessed right with one of the gallery's most difficult patrons. She imagined a scene in which Alex congratulated her for not letting Myra's bad temper intimidate her. In her other daydreams she fell asleep and woke up in his arms; sometimes her visions were so realistic, she could catch a whiff of his favorite after-shave and feel the tingle of his caress down her spine.

She invited the neighbor with the gray poodle in for coffee and dessert, discovering that she was a recent widow very much at a loss about rebuilding her life. On a rainy Sunday she shared a cab with the young newlyweds from across the hall, finding them as charming as they were playful. The city was beginning to seem less lonely.

The American wing of the Met distracted her for most of one Saturday afternoon, and she allowed herself the luxury of a long call to her parents. She gave them a wealth of details about her job and apartment; but when her mother's questions about her social life began to hit close to home, Kate ended the conversation. She was surviving, even thriving.

Alex had been gone for two weeks, but everything about him was fresh in her mind: the tiny scar on his left temple from a rough game of hockey, the ridge of calluses on his palms caused by weight lifting during his weekly workouts, the prominent little bump on his nose. Somehow his minor imperfections were more endearing than his assets: a lean, powerful build, a strong jaw and chin, and his inborn grace.

Blanche found Kate on the third floor Monday morning,

141

approaching with none of her usual matter-of-fact friendliness.

"I don't know why Alex didn't want to talk to you," she began apologetically.

"Probably you were handier." Kate wished she could believe that.

"Anyway, he's decided to stay in Amsterdam a while longer. Heaven only knows, he needs a vacation. When the gallery is closed in August, he usually spends all his time working at the Candlebrook warehouse getting ready for the new season."

"How much longer?" Kate asked. Making her question sound casual took the acting skill of a Barrymore.

"He didn't say."

Blanche's hesitancy was making Kate very nervous.

"What did he say?"

"He wanted me to make plane reservations on the first available flight to Amsterdam. For you."

"For me?" Kate could remember word for word Alex's statement about needing her at the gallery, not on the buying trip. "Did he say why?"

"Only that it was urgent to the future of your professional association."

"I don't believe it," Kate said more to herself than to the secretary.

"Well, I was surprised too. I mean, Nancy can handle the retail sales, but you've been so busy the last two weeks. I checked with the airport. I can pick up a cancellation for you on a KLM flight tomorrow if I call back right away. You do have a valid passport?"

"Yes, but I'm not sure . . ."

"Is Alex hinting that he'll let you go if you don't join him in Amsterdam?" Blanche couldn't conceal her anxiety. "This isn't like him."

"You took his call. Is he?"

"I'm not sure. He's usually pretty direct, but he said

something about doing you a favor if I persuaded you to go. Kate, I don't want to push you into something you don't want to do."

"You won't be."

"Should I make a reservation?"

"Not yet. I have to think about it."

"This is the busy season for European flights. I should call right back if there's any chance at all that you want to go."

She'd been in a state of suspended animation, frantically going through the motions of living while her mind was constantly on Alex. Rushing to Amsterdam because Alex wanted her there would be a turning point in her life. More likely than not, it would mark the end of both her job and her faltering relationship with him. One thing was sure: She couldn't go on indefinitely, obsessed with love for him but without any hope of a future together.

"Book the flight," she said grimly. Her father would call it taking the bull by the horns.

How could she pack when the purpose and length of her trip were a total mystery? Somehow she threw together a caseful of her least wrinkly clothes and enough toiletries to last through the week, adding comfortable sandals for walking and a pair of dressy white heels. Remembering how carefully she'd planned and packed for her short tourist jaunt to Britain, she laughed a little hysterically. Her last chore before getting into bed was calling her parents. They were thrilled for her.

By six A.M. she'd given up on sleep, wondering if she'd dozed three hours during the whole night. After checking in an hour early at the airport, she wandered about like a zombie, feeling more like a patient about to go in for surgery than a carefree traveler. Maybe meeting Alex would be a kind of surgical procedure, in which her heart would be dissected and part of it left with him forever. She bought him a silly key holder that said The Key to My Heart, then gave

143

it instead to a little boy waiting in a passenger area with his mother.

By the time she boarded the Royal Dutch Airlines plane, she was exhausted enough to sleep during most of the flight. Schiphol Airport was busy but very orderly, with shops offering Bols Genever—the famous Dutch gin her father would love to try—along with perfume, cigars, watches, radios, and other gifts. She had to change her dollars to guilders before she could think about presents to take home, but she felt more like crying as she walked along dejectedly, watching men who weren't Alex pass her by.

Damn it, it was his idea for her to come to Amsterdam. Where was he?

Then she spotted him. In a gray suit and looking slimmer than she remembered, he hurried toward her oblivious to the interested female glances that followed him.

"Kate, I'm sorry. Your plane was early."

"No, I think it was right on time." She hadn't flown across the ocean to be fooled.

He picked up her large bag, moving swiftly through the terminal and depositing her in a waiting taxi.

"Have you had dinner?" They might have been casual friends meeting for reasons of convenience.

"On the plane, yes."

"A good flight?"

"Very smooth."

"I fly a lot, but I don't enjoy it."

"I imagine turbulence bothers you."

He frowned at her. "Not as much as carnival rides."

The driver whisked them through the twilight, making a few comments in excellent English. Alex said nothing, and she refused to ask the only question that mattered: Why did he want her there?

"I found a room for you at the Museum Hotel, right near the Rijksmuseum. Accommodations are scarce this time of the year."

144

"That's where you're staying?"

"No, I always stay at a small hotel, not fancy, but the people there were great on my first buying trip when I had to watch every penny. Unfortunately, they didn't have a vacancy for you."

She had a quick impression of a somewhat wedge-shaped building and corner windows with small window boxes blooming with flowers on the second and third stories. Alex carried her luggage and checked her in, giving her little time to take in the surroundings. She followed him up the stairs to the second floor. Kate was impressed by the coziness of the place, with its elegant tall clock and a patterned rug on the floor.

"This is a *pension,* a nice family hotel," Alex said, setting her bag inside a small but pleasant room with simple wooden furnishings. "Breakfast comes with the room. Shall I meet you here around nine o'clock?"

"You're leaving?" It was stupid to ask; he obviously was.

"I'll see you tomorrow," he said, handing her the room key as though she might miss it if he laid it on the dresser.

Incredible as it seemed, he left her.

Just like that! she said to herself, stunned, disappointed, and agitated.

Not even her wildest fantasies had led her to hope he would sweep her into his arms and swear undying love, but this reception was ludicrous. He had arrived late at the airport and had then practically dumped her in a strange room in a foreign city without giving her the slightest hint why she was there. She didn't know whether to scream, cry, or try to get back to the airport to book the next possible flight home.

The room was impressively clean, with plastic covering the lower part of the patterned wallpaper. The bed was softer than she was used to, with huge down pillows in ironed cotton cases. The bathroom, she soon discovered, was down the hall; there would be an extra charge for the bath.

What on earth was she doing alone in an Amsterdam

145

hotel room? She could learn to hate the man who'd so unceremoniously abandoned her there.

The next morning she did hate him, but breakfast cheered her. The people in the dining room were friendly, hospitable, and English-speaking, serving her along with a group of American students and a scattering of other tourists. The rolls that made up the standard continental breakfast had hard, crusty exteriors and warm, yeasty centers; they were served with plenty of butter, which was less salted than American butter, and an array of jams. The tea came steaming hot, although cooler than her temper when she thought of Alex. He could have said something before running off last night!

If he was two minutes late by her watch, now reset to Amsterdam time, she would strike off on her own to see the city and let him wonder where she was. In fact, he was ten minutes early and found her still lingering over a cup of tea.

"Are you ready to see the sights?" he asked, seeming almost shy as he led her out to the street.

"No, I'm not." She felt stubborn, slighted, and uncooperative.

"You want to know why I sent for you?" he asked with resignation.

"Is that what you did, send for me?"

"I begged Blanche to persuade you to come, if you want to know the truth."

"Yes, I want to know the truth."

"I missed you."

A pair of Japanese tourists passed them, aiming their cameras at the gorgeous boxes of flowers above their heads.

Alex had given the one answer that could disarm her.

"Then why did you run off so fast last night?"

"Was the room all right?" He sounded anxious but didn't answer her question.

"Yes. Very clean. Fine."

"Good." He took her arm.

146

"Tell me, Alex. Why did you leave so soon?"

"I thought you'd be tired after the flight."

"Not too tired for a few minutes of conversation!"

"No." He just didn't sound like himself.

"Alex, I don't understand any of this!" She lowered her voice, aware of the curious glances of some passing students. "Why are you being so evasive?"

"Do you"—he spoke so softly she had to strain to hear the words—"have any idea how much I wanted to stay in your room last night? I lay awake half the night imagining you snuggled in a nest of those fluffy pillows. Miss you! I just couldn't trust myself to stay!"

His grip on her fingers was painful, but it told her even more than his words.

"I missed you too." Her voice was a pathetic whimper, but he responded by putting an arm around her shoulders.

"The best way to see Amsterdam is on foot. Do you mind walking?" he asked.

"I love walking."

He missed her! For now that was enough.

Maybe because she was so much in love with Alex, she immediately fell in love with the city they were sharing. Concentric canals ringed Amsterdam, crossed by streets that radiated out like the spokes of a wheel. The heart of the city, Old Amsterdam, was a tourists' paradise with its crooked cobbled streets, fairy-tale rooflines, and nooks and crannies to explore on every hand. The seventeenth-century houses were especially picturesque. The false fronts of these narrow brick structures rose high above the actual roofs of the houses.

"They built narrow fronts because taxes then were determined by the amount of frontage. They made up for it by making the houses deep with private gardens in back," Alex said.

"Why the false fronts on top with no building behind them?"

147

"The higher the house, the more prestige."

"Compensation for the land being so flat?"

"A good guess."

Window boxes were everywhere, and Alex bought her a nosegay of red and yellow blooms at a flower stall. He was patient while she explored the Kalverstraat shops. Several times he offered to buy things for her but accepted her refusals. They came upon delightful boutiques in little alleys, and Kate found herself tempted by everything from costume dolls to wooden shoes and Delft pottery but was reluctant to rush into making purchases.

"How long will we be here?" she asked, wondering whether to have some tulip bulbs sent to her mother.

"Long enough."

He was still being maddeningly evasive, but sharing the city hand in hand with him made her more tranquil. She couldn't entice him into an Indonesian restaurant, but he did agree to a lunch of *broodjes*, bread rolls with delicious fillings. She tried the eel, finding it a little too salty, but he insisted on ham and cheese. They sat at an outdoor café watching the people and drinking Dutch beer, enjoying each other.

Their afternoon passed quickly at the Rijksmuseum, although in such a short time they couldn't possibly see all the collections housed in that vast red Victorian structure. Awestruck as all art lovers are by Rembrandt's huge *Night Watch*, they were content to absorb its beauty and artistry without intellectualizing it. Kate was especially interested in the dollhouse collection, but Alex seemed to spend most of his time watching her—to her confusion and delight.

After a dinner of *biefstuk*, exceptional rare beef that pleased them both, taken in the cozy atmosphere that seemed to be a Dutch specialty, they took a canal tour by candlelight, nibbling on cheese and getting more tipsy on their feelings for each other than on the wine as the boat slid past an enchanted city of gabled houses.

Too stimulated to feel tired, they went to a nightclub, where they drank *jenever,* a lemon gin, and danced until it became a form of exquisite torture to hold each other close. She was sure Alex wouldn't leave her alone this night.

They came into the hotel laughing, quieting when a stout dark-haired woman scowled at them with scolding eyes. The other guests seemed to have bedded down earlier, giving the hotel the deserted look of an off-season resort. Kate made a necessary trek down the hall, giving Alex her key.

The room was dimly lit, and Alex was staring out the single-curtained window, one without a gay flower box below it.

"I'll go now if you say so," he said hoarsely, without turning to face her.

"I had a wonderful time today—and tonight," she said evasively.

"That sounds like my cue to exit."

She longed for him to stay but didn't want to say so. If he would look at her, words would be unnecessary.

"No," she finally had to whisper.

"I don't know if I'm a heel or a fool!" he said in a vehement outburst, turning toward her.

"Do you want me to decide which?" She sank down on the edge of the bed, studying the white embossed cotton spread.

"No, don't." He sat beside her, not touching, staring at his thumbnail. "You shouldn't have come."

"You wouldn't have fired me?"

He didn't catch the teasing in her voice. "Is that what you thought? Katie"—he gripped her hands in exasperation—"that's crazy!"

"Blanche said something about our professional association."

"Could I tell my secretary why I really wanted you here?"

"No, but you can tell me."

149

"I can't believe," he said, drawing her into his arms, "that I haven't kissed you all day."

He more than made up for lost time, hungrily covering her mouth with his, not sparing her lips, thrusting his tongue toward the base of hers. Shaky and weak, she pulled away, knowing the deep satisfaction his body could give her but needing more, much more.

"Alex, I know I'm not here to buy antiques."

"No, I arranged for several container loads a week ago," he said.

"Are you going to make me ask again?"

"No." He stood and pulled her into his arms. "You're here because I missed you more than I could believe possible. I didn't think it could happen to a crusty old bachelor, but I'm falling in love with you, Katie."

Burying her face against his shoulder to hide watery eyes, she could only hug him with all her strength, scarcely daring to believe his hesitant declaration.

"Hey, look at me, darling. I love you. I really do love you." He tested the words like a man sampling an exotic brew, then whispered once again, "I love you, Katie."

He tilted her chin and kissed her in a long, lingering union of their mouths, full of patience and promise.

"I don't know if this is a double-occupancy room," she teased, glancing at the bed, an odd size somewhere between a single and a double.

"It is. I registered as Mr. and Mrs. Gilbert."

"You didn't!" She broke free, evading his hands as he tried to pull her back. "Do you know how cocky and conceited you sound? Do you—"

"Yes."

There was nowhere to run; the bed was flush with the wall on the far side, and Alex was blocking the door.

"I know why you're down on romance! You don't know the first thing about conducting one!" Short of moving the heavy wooden dresser and hiding behind it, there was no place to go.

"Don't I get any points for a candle-lit canal ride?" He stood a few feet away, enjoying the game of cat and mouse as much as she was.

"You were more interested in the wine than in me."

"Wrong! I needed to get a little tipsy to admit how much I love you."

"You don't love me when you're sober?"

"Of course I do, you unprincipled tease!" He dropped his voice to a whisper. "But if you don't believe me, I'm more than ready to fall asleep."

"Then go to your own hotel."

"I'm too tired to bother." He slipped out of his navy jacket, dropping it on a plain wooden chair—the only one in the room—and slowly unbuttoned his white shirt.

His belt clanked on the floor as slacks fell to his feet, and he turned his back to remove socks and shorts, tossing the rest of his garments on top of the jacket and moving slowly toward the bed.

He couldn't possibly know how the expanse of his back, golden in the muted lighting, made her want to feel the firm swells and ridges of his body. His buttocks were round and muscular, excitingly masculine. Neatly folding the spread and laying it on the dresser, he kept the angle of his back toward her, then crawled between crisp muslin sheets, resting his head on the pillow farthest from the wall.

"Good night, darling," he murmured, feigning a sleepiness that was wholly unbelievable.

"You're in my place," she said, unbuttoning her own wrinkle-proof navy skirt, not caring that it fell to the dust-free floor.

"There's plenty of room on the other side."

"I'm not going to crawl over you to get there."

"No?" He propped himself up on one elbow, watching her

undress. The amused intensity of his gaze made her hesitate self-consciously and decide to leave her underwear on.

"This is my room," she insisted. "Either move over or go to your own hotel."

He did move to the far side, watching while she adjusted the window to a half-open position.

"Leave the light on," he ordered.

"It will keep me awake."

"No, it won't."

His expression was mellow, his eyes beseeching. She didn't hesitate any longer, knowing that she had become his the moment she told Blanche to make her plane reservation. The weather was cool at night in the Low Country, with a hint of rain in the air. She shivered and slid under the sheet, knowing that no blanket would be needed to keep warm this night. The clean-smelling cotton fabric felt stiff when she bunched it against her face.

"Are you trying to hide from me?" He turned on his side and ran a single finger from her forehead to her chin, easily whisking away the sheet.

"Should I?"

"Not if you love me." His voice was soft but urgent.

"That's the trouble. I do."

"Oh, Katie." He leaned over her, slowly bestowing an innocent kiss on her parted lips.

Her head sunk into the downy depths of the pillow as Alex explored her face with the gentlest of touches.

"Have you ever slept on pillows like these?" he asked, sliding his leg over hers and leaning an elbow beside her head. "One's pricking my arm."

He reached under the edge of the case and found the hard quill of the offending feather, working it through the cotton covering until one fluffy white feather was clasped between his fingers.

"Imagine how many of these it takes to fill one case," he said, laying it aside on his pillow and kissing her again and again—long, sweet kisses that encouraged her to flick her tongue between the hard edges of his teeth.

"How can a woman who wears cotton panties accuse me of not being romantic?" he teased, fondling her breasts under the layer of practical white tricot, then slowly edging the straps over her shoulders. After he tossed aside her bra, she wiggled out of her panties, torn between wanting his unhurried lovemaking to go on forever and needing to feel him thrusting deep within her.

He cupped one breast with both hands, arousing her nipple, then he covered it with his lips and caressed it with his tongue until her groin throbbed. Glad now that the light was on, she watched his face, otherworldly in his passion, and let her hands wander, unwilling to stop when he restrained her intimate explorations.

"Not yet," he whispered, placing her hands beside her own body and reaching for the loose feather on his pillow.

He ran the delicate tip of the feather over her ears and throat, stilling the ticklish sensation with his mouth and tongue, trailing it over the hollows under her arms and down her ribs, saving her from a fit of giggles with the pressure of his lips. Her breasts ached under the merciless assault of the feather until they were suckled; then once again he tormented them with the almost weightless fluff.

Wiggling in desperation, she watched the white instrument bedevil her navel and flicker downward, creating a sensation that Alex skillfully heightened until she cried out in shock, rocked by wave after wave of delicious sensations.

Mindless with joy, she grasped at him, meeting his first thrust with abandoned desire. They moved together rhythmically, lost in a haze of sharp, pleasurable sensations. With one great burst of energy they linked themselves together, scaled the highest peaks, and collapsed, speechless and transformed.

Later she found the poor bent feather, testing its devilish tip on his tiny brown nipples and hair-sprinkled skin, making him shudder for mercy, which she willingly granted on her own terms.

Sometime in the night it rained, and when Alex closed the window, he turned off the light, returning to find her nestled on her tummy on a mound of pillows. She awoke that way at dawn with Alex's arm across her shoulders and his leg nudging her bottom. For two people who had everything in the world to talk about, they found very little time to say anything.

The next day was the kind honeymooners dream of but seldom achieve. Their day began with lunch at one of Amsterdam's many brown cafés, a smoky wooden-walled pub off a cobbled street. Their sandwiches were a Dutch specialty that not even Alex objected to: thick slices of bread with roast beef and cheese, each slice topped by three fried eggs. They drank Dutch beer. That afternoon they wandered about soaking up the sounds and smells of the still rainy byways. Finding to their own amazement that they wanted tea before five o'clock, they sipped uncounted cups and ate crunchy biscuits Alex insisted on calling cookies.

Deciding no two humans needed another meal that day, they shared strawberries and *kernhem,* a soft, creamy cheese, at another café instead of eating dinner and didn't even consider sampling more of the city's notorious night life.

"I wish we could stay here forever," Kate purred against his shoulder when they snuggled together in bed.

"So do I." He kissed her temples and eyelids, unhurriedly caressing her.

Surprised again by the sudden urgency that sprang up between them, they made joyful, uninhibited love ending with a pillow fight that left them flushed and breathless.

"I like you," he said, trapping her against his chest in self-defense.

"You said you loved me." She pretended to pout, too secure at this moment to think about the day when they would go home.

"That too."

The room was sunny, but chill air from the window he thrust open made her pull the sheet over her shoulders and bury her face in the pillow.

"Up and at 'em."

He whipped away the thin covering and planted a playful slap on her exposed derrière, laughing at her sleepy outrage.

"Up and at what?"

"It's a beautiful day for a bike tour."

That meant they weren't going home that day. Any suggestion that lengthened their stay brightened her day. The only shadow in this wonderland of love was their mutual reluctance to plan ahead. Like Cinderella at the ball, Kate couldn't imagine a greater happiness beyond that moment.

Neither had packed jeans; in fact, Alex's clothes, sent over from his other room, were all appropriate for business: jackets, slacks, and a tan suit. He wore navy slacks with a short-sleeved oxford-cloth shirt; though the button-down collar was an unlikely style for biking along the dikes, the color was flattering to his dark good looks. He gambled on good weather and left his jacket in the room. Kate had to settle for pale blue slacks and a navy knit shirt but took along her white sweater.

They rented bikes in the middle of Amsterdam, joining a guided tour of mostly students who raced through the congested streets with nonchalant disregard for life or limb. Kate and Alex brought up the rear, feeling alone even in a group. Neither had done much bike riding since college, but once safely beyond the city, the tour started to seem like a wonderful jaunt.

Dikes, Kate discovered, were little rivers or big ditches with earth built up on either side. It was possible to cycle on top of one, looking down from the dirt path on a *polder,* land reclaimed from the sea. The flatness of the land made riding

155

easy. She was thrilled to see real windmills on the landscape, not at all disillusioned when their guide said modern technology had replaced their functions.

The land was made for cycling with clearly marked *fietspaden,* or bike paths. They passed a farmer wearing yellow wooden shoes and clusters of neat brick homes with the ever-lovely window boxes.

"You're beautiful," Alex whispered when they stopped for lunch, and at that moment she believed it might be true.

At lunch Alex indulged his sweet tooth with *poffertjes,* small round pancakes topped with butter and a dusting of sugar, and sweet spiced *koek,* or cake. Leaving the quaint village restaurant with the boisterous group of students, Kate had the oddest feeling, as though nothing that was happening were real. Her disorientation lasted only a few seconds, then Alex took her hand as they walked to their bikes. Knowing she shouldn't let it disturb her, she still found the trip back less enthralling, wondering if she would ever be so happy again.

With sore seats and aching calves, they were more than satisfied with a quiet dinner at the hotel, going to bed early and falling asleep easily after gently making love.

His travel alarm surprised her, sounding when the room was still a murky gray. Dashing to the dresser to turn it off, she found that dawn, not rainy weather, accounted for the dimness in the room.

"You set your clock?" She shivered and reached in her suitcase for a nightgown.

"Afraid so. Come back to bed for a few minutes."

"Why?"

"I'll show you why." He patted the empty space beside him.

"No. Why did you set the alarm?"

"We've got to stop playing hooky, darling." He didn't sound as lighthearted as he'd intended.

"We're leaving?"

"Afraid so."

"When did you decide to leave today?"

"When I asked you to come here."

"Ordered me to come."

He ignored that. "When I knew you were coming, I booked return seats."

"Why today?"

"Today was available. Summer flights are well booked."

"Tomorrow wasn't?"

"I didn't know how hard it would be to leave. But we're going back together, Katie."

"Yes."

She couldn't give any reason for feeling so apprehensive, but she had a firm conviction that nothing would ever be quite as wonderful as the last days had been.

"There are things we can do at home that we can't do here," he said, sitting up in bed and still inviting her with his eyes.

"Work?"

"No, play. I want to serenade you in bed. Have you ever had a naked man play the mandolin for you?"

"That will be novel," she said dryly.

"And you might consider going on the pill. I don't mind being responsible for that, but . . ."

"Maybe," she said, pretending to hunt through her suitcase.

Alex expected their lovemaking to go on; she, too, would be devastated if it didn't. But where did that leave them? Going back to New York meant facing conflicts she'd deliberately ignored in Amsterdam. He loved her, but he was as uncommitted as before. If eventually she was going to lose him, wouldn't it be better to do it now while she was still young enough to build another kind of life?

The thought of life without Alex made her want to weep.

"Darling, don't look like it's the end of the world." He

came up behind her and drew her against his bare torso, patting her hair. "Even the greatest vacations have to end."

"Yes, I know." She pressed her face against his chest, wishing they were prisoners in the little room, unable to run away from their love.

"I've never been happier," he whispered.

He carried her back to bed, not needing to rush because he had, as usual, planned well when he set the clock. They had hours to enjoy before their plane left.

CHAPTER NINE

They flew into a summer thunderstorm with upper-air turbulence that made Alex slump in his seat in abject misery.
Kate held his hand and offered useless suggestions until she
sensed he was more annoyed than comforted. The landing
was bumpy, making her even more anxious for him and
more than willing to be one of the last passengers to disem-
bark. He sat there fighting his airsickness, finally leaving
with an exaggerated pretense that everything was fine.

The formalities of checking through customs were doubly
irksome because Alex so obviously felt awful, and their
driver, who must have apprenticed at the Indianapolis 500,
raced the cab through the still drizzly streets on springs that
offered as much cushioning as a buckboard wagon. Kate
insisted that the taxi go to Alex's apartment first; he didn't
even make a token protest. In front of her own apartment
she paid the driver with a twenty—Alex had never let her
change her dollars to guilders—and found herself on the
pavement with a heavy suitcase to lug up three flights.

"Welcome home, Kate," she said aloud, but it wasn't
Alex's airsickness, the weather, or the trek to the third floor
that depressed her.

The studio apartment was stuffy, but the damp breeze that
came through the window didn't seem to freshen it. She
unpacked, straightened up a bit, and bathed, then crawled
onto her hide-a-bed blaming jet lag for her restlessness when
she found herself still awake an hour later. Of course, Alex

was much too ill to talk about their future; nausea was poison to romance. She had to believe that what they'd shared in Amsterdam was too special and important not to change both their lives. Why, then, was she so uncertain and insecure? She loved Alex and truly believed in his love for her. Maybe in the morning he would sweep aside all her doubts and lay out a glorious future for both of them—together.

Glad for the brief weekend respite before returning to work, she cleaned her apartment, did the laundry, and waited for Alex's call. It was nearly noon before it came.

"I'm not an ideal traveling companion," he joked.

"That's true. How are you feeling now?"

"Fine. I'm never sick on solid ground. I do have bad news, though."

In her present mood any other kind of news would have surprised her.

"My manager at Candlebrook had a heart attack, a mild one, but I think his wife is going to use it as a lever to get him to retire to Florida."

"So you're going to run the warehouse yourself?" She wondered drearily whether this meant another frustrating separation.

"No, he has a nephew who's interested in the business and has some experience. I'm going there now to meet him."

"Oh."

"I want you to come along."

"When are you leaving?"

"I'll pick you up in about half an hour. Bring an overnight bag. I don't think I'll bother driving back tonight."

"I haven't said I'll go." It was a technicality, but she didn't want to be taken for granted.

"Will you?"

"What will I do there?"

"Keep me company."

"I suppose it's the best offer I'll get today."

160

"It damn well better be!"

"I need at least forty-five minutes."

"You've got them."

The warehouse was a converted barn on the outskirts of what was little more than a village, convenient to the turnpike and only a short drive from the tree-shaded business district. Alex had sold off most of the acreage but kept the old farmhouse as a residence for his manager. He rented a tiny apartment in town for his own use on frequent trips to Candlebrook.

"This is the foundation of my financial empire," he said, stopping the station wagon in front of a massive gray barn. "My grandfather left it to me, and it seemed an ideal place to wholesale antiques. Not too far from large cities and not too costly to maintain."

"Your grandfather was a farmer?"

"No, a banker. He bought the property on speculation and leased it."

"Too bad." She liked the idea of Alex as a little boy playing in the hayloft on his grandparents' farm.

The inside of the barn seemed even larger, with crowded rows of furniture completely filling the board floor on the ground level. Wide stairs, obviously newer than the rest of the structure, led to a full second story with thousands of smaller items arranged in cases and on tables. The stock was mostly Victorian or later, with a quantity of mission oak and even a few better pieces of blond furniture from the mid-twentieth century.

"Not the kind of thing we display at the gallery," Alex said, guessing at her reaction, "but the bread-and-butter part of my business."

"This is what we sell in Nebraska. I feel right at home."

Fine old furniture of any era had its own merits, she decided. Was selling a Colonial highboy really that much more exciting than finding a buyer for a round oak table? Now she

161

wasn't as sure about the answer as she'd been a few months ago.

"I wish I didn't have an interview." He took her in his arms, giving her a long-overdue kiss.

"Then we wouldn't be here, would we?" She linked her fingers behind his neck, mussing the back of his hair with her thumbs.

"I'll have to show him through this place and then the house, because the use of it comes with the job. I made a few calls, and he sounds like a good prospect, so the interview will take awhile." He kissed her again, loosening his hold with obvious reluctance.

"I can entertain myself unless there's something you want me to do."

"No, we sell everything here as is, mostly by the truck or van load. No researching, no guarantees, but I work hard keeping the quality high."

"Will all the Dutch stuff be sold here?"

"About ninety percent."

"I'll just wander around, maybe take a walk if your interview lasts a long time."

"We'll have a nice dinner. I know an old inn with fireplaces in every room. You can order *escargots,* clams, oysters, anything fishy."

"What will you eat?"

"I'll force myself to try the lobster tail."

"Why do I feel I'm being bribed?"

"Because you are." He kissed the end of her nose and made it itch.

Over dinner they would talk, she assured herself, wondering how she would feel about living with Alex without being married. It wasn't what she wanted, but not being with him continuously seemed like a new version of purgatory. The dry, dusty odor in the poorly ventilated barn eventually drove her outside, where she wandered down a blacktopped country road until the sun felt uncomfortably hot and her

162

feet hurt. Walking back down the graded stone driveway to the barn, she saw an extremely tall, painfully thin young man with bright red hair getting into a pickup truck by the entrance. Moments later Alex came out to meet her, looking pleased.

"How did it go?"

"Good. He has auction barn experience and worked for a show promoter for several years. I have a few more references to check, but I think I'll offer him the job."

"Does that mean you'll have to say here until then?"

"No, we're closed on Mondays. I can come back Tuesday to help break him in. Doris is a whiz, so there's no real worry."

"Why don't you make her manager?"

"Are you suggesting I'm practicing sexual discrimination?" he asked mockingly.

"Are you?"

"I've offered her the manager's job three times."

"Why doesn't she take it?"

"With four kids, a three-day workweek is almost more than she wants. Full time is out."

Kate wondered if she had as much to learn about Alex as she did about his Candlebrook business. In the back of her mind was a nagging little annoyance: He seemed to leak out bits of information instead of telling her everything at once. How did he feel now about being with her? He said he loved her, but did it mean the same thing to him as it did to her?

Dinner was delicious, the inn was charming, but Kate didn't enjoy any of it. Alex talked about the craze for golden oak, his parents' trip to Hong Kong, and the frustrations of trying to get government permission to export antiques from France.

"A Paris auction is bedlam compared with ours, but can you believe, there's a thirty-year guarantee against misrepresentation. Someday we'll go on an auction trip: England, Germany, Switzerland, maybe Austria or Monaco."

163

"We?" She picked at a frog leg, wondering if she had ordered the chickenlike delicacy just because Alex wrinkled his nose in distaste when she read a description of it from the menu.

"You're my administrative assistant. Your expenses are tax deductible too."

This wasn't what she wanted to hear.

She had never faked a headache in her life, but there was a first time for everything, as her father often said when trying to cajole bidders into buying an especially bizarre item.

"I have some aspirin at my apartment," Alex said sympathetically. "Maybe if you take a couple and lie down, you'll feel better."

"Alex, I really would like to go home."

"Back to New York tonight?"

"You said there's no need to be here until Tuesday."

"Yes, but I thought we could stay overnight and drive back in the morning. Late in the morning."

She knew exactly what he had thought, but more and more she rebelled against being his sleep-over date. What had been so inevitable in Amsterdam now seemed anything but romantic.

Late at night, lying on the couch because she didn't want to be alone on the double expanse of the hide-a-bed, she yearned to have him, on any terms.

In the morning her headache was real, worse than the one she had pretended to have. She blamed the storm clouds gathering over the city but secretly believed that she was being punished for lying to Alex instead of telling him how she really felt. When he called before noon to ask how her head felt, her fib caught up with her. A headache two days in a row hardly seemed plausible, so she spent a miserable afternoon at his apartment watching a tennis match on TV, listening to him play several different instruments, and pretending to feel fine.

164

"You're not kidding me, you know," he said as they shared an onion-and-pepper omelet for dinner.

"About what?" Did she sound as guilty as she felt?

"How you feel. If those black shadows under your eyes are any indication, you still have a headache."

"Actually, I do."

"You should've said something. I give marvelous neck massages."

"Your talents never cease to amaze me, but I think it's only the weather."

The threatened storm still hadn't come. Was the weather over Manhattan always so ominous?

"Sit here," he ordered, pointing at a low stool he used for playing his guitar.

"I really don't think—"

"Sit!"

"You don't have to be bossy." She sat stiffly on the sheepskin seat.

His claim wasn't just bragging; he massaged the rigid muscles of her neck and shoulders with penetrating gentleness, working out kinks and knots she hadn't been aware of. A warm feeling of well-being spread down her back, making the pain in her temples much more bearable.

"How's your head now?" He got down on his knees and faced her, pressing his fingertips softly into the bony little hollows at the corners of her eyes.

"It really is better. Thank you."

"Don't sound so surprised." He leaned forward and kissed her but didn't press for a response. "I'm going to put you to bed now."

"I can't stay here. Tomorrow's a workday, and I can't go to the gallery in these slacks."

"You can't stay here, because you wouldn't get any sleep if you did. I'll drive you home and tuck you in."

The sky opened up as he approached her block. The parking situation was as hopeless as usual. Over his protests she insisted that he drop her at her door and then continue on home rather than circle the block to find an empty space and get soaked running back. Since the windshield wipers were totally ineffective in such a deluge, he reluctantly had to kiss her good night, unhurried by the honking of an impatient driver behind him.

She started crying on reaching the second flight of stairs and didn't stop until her eyes ached more than her head. A wonderful man claimed to love her; why couldn't she let things take a leisurely course without torturing herself? Nothing mattered but mutual love and respect; a wedding was no guarantee of either. She had always known that Alex would not surrender his independence, certainly not for the romance he scorned. Why couldn't she be satisfied with what she had?

Cried out at last, she felt an uneasy peace. There was no way she could stop loving Alex. Her life was like a roller-coaster ride with its tremendous highs and nerve-racking plunges. What could she do besides stay on for the full trip? Leaving Alex was as unthinkable as forcing him into something he didn't want.

He must love me; he must love me. She fell asleep only partly comforted by this refrain.

She went to work the next morning feeling fragile; fast movements and disturbing thoughts threatened to shatter her skull, but as long as she moved slowly and avoided conflict, there was a chance of survival. Alex helped by disappearing for the day and later leaving for Connecticut after a quick dinner they shared at a lunch counter.

"I wish I didn't need you so much," he said, seeing her to the bus stop in the still-light evening.

She didn't answer.

"At the gallery, I mean." He gave her a quick kiss. "I'd love to take you with me."

"That would make Mrs. Winthrop Davis very cross, I'm afraid. We have an appointment tomorrow."

"You're doing a spectacular job, darling. My clients are beginning to prefer you, I think."

"Tell me that after I sell the Belter set."

"I will. I'll miss you."

"Me too." She boarded the bus, unable to see if Alex watched it pull away from the curb.

He stayed a second night in Candlebrook, calling to remind her that they hadn't made love since Amsterdam.

"Are you coming back tomorrow?" she asked, almost embarrassed by the eagerness behind her question.

"It doesn't look good. My new manager has a lot to learn."

"He'll work out all right?"

"I'm sure he will. I'm just impatient to be back with you."

"Me too." She hung up wondering why everything she said seemed so inadequate.

When Blanche transferred the call to the third floor, Kate was practically standing on her head while examining the legs of a chest.

"Kate, it's me," the caller said.

"Bill? Where are you?"

"In Washington, D.C., my boss thinks. I didn't think a little stopover in the Big Apple would rock the meat-packing industry."

"You're at the airport?"

"No, at the Blackstone Hotel. Thought I'd better check in. Can I pick you up at work?"

"I don't know."

"I have to see you, Kate."

Seeing him was the least she could do, unwise as it seemed.

"I'm nearly done. Maybe you should meet me at my apartment in, say, an hour."

"That'll be fine."

It would be terrible, not fine. There was nothing she could say to Bill that wouldn't make him unhappy. He had been a

167

friend when she badly needed one, but what man who thought he was in love wanted to be called a good buddy?

He was standing on the front stoop of her building gallantly opening the door for Kate's new friend the widow, his jacket hanging over one arm that looked beefy in a short-sleeved yellow shirt. His hair was baby-fine and almost white, but the bright sun did terrible things to his skin, giving it a burned-all-over glow. Why was such a decent, likable man compelled to hang around on the streets of New York waiting for a woman who didn't want him? Weren't there all kinds of sweet, sunny-dispositioned girls in Iowa who would adore making a home for him? Why her?

Not much liking herself at the moment, she squared her shoulders, sucked in her stomach and buttocks, and marched up to face him.

"It's good to see you," he said softly.

She wanted to kick herself, but she couldn't say the same thing to him.

"Let's go upstairs."

She deliberately ran up the stairs, but he kept up, puffing just a little on the top landing.

"I guess you're used to steps," he said.

"People can get used to lots of things."

Inside the door, she couldn't hold back. "You shouldn't have come, Bill."

"I know that. You haven't given me any false hopes, that's for sure." He dropped his jacket on the platform rocker and sat down on the couch. "I guess I was hoping you wouldn't look so good. Like maybe my memory was playing tricks on me. I don't even have a picture of you."

"You don't want one, Bill. It's so much better if you forget me."

"At least have dinner with me."

"But there's no point!"

"We are friends?"

"Of course."

168

"I'll feel silly going to a Japanese restaurant all by myself. I may have to take my shoes off."

"Holes in your socks?"

"I hope not. If you're with me, it won't matter. No one will notice my big feet one way or another."

"I'm sure you can leave your shoes on."

"Come with me anyway."

"Bill, I don't—"

"Just dinner. I won't even get out of the cab afterward. Please."

She wanted to refuse but didn't. Dinner didn't go too badly except for one stormy moment.

"One thing I've had on my mind," he said, uncharacteristically picking at his shrimp. "Is there someone else?"

"Yes." It was hard to admit it, but there was no point in lying.

"That boss of yours?"

"Yes."

"Is he going to marry you?"

"I don't think so." Saying the truth out loud made it seem much worse.

"Damn it, Kate, he's not for you! You're too nice a girl to stay in this city just to hang around him!"

"He doesn't much like you either."

"He'll like me a lot less after I mop the floor with his face!"

"And that would make everything all right?" She wasn't being sarcastic.

"No," he admitted grudgingly. "But I don't understand. Why him?"

"I don't know."

They said good-bye in the cab, sadly and quietly. His kiss on her forehead was oddly comforting.

"I'll never forget you," he said sadly.

There were never any parking spaces on her street, never! Yet, against all odds, the station wagon across the street

169

looked terribly familiar. Pretending not to see it, she sprinted up the steps and into the building, not slowing until she was inside her apartment. She couldn't be positive Alex had been behind the wheel, but she wasn't left in suspense for long.

"Is it my turn?" Alex asked angrily when she gathered up enough courage to respond to the buzzer.

"Alex?"

"Are you going to let me in?"

"Yes." She couldn't imagine keeping him out.

His face was cold and hard, making him look older even though he was still wearing the casual slacks and knit shirt he preferred at Candlebrook.

"You have no reason to be angry," she said.

"Then why didn't you wait for me on the street?"

It was below her dignity to pretend she hadn't seen the station wagon.

"I wasn't expecting you this early."

"So you ran away from me?"

"I wasn't thinking."

"Not of me anyway." He closed the door and circled the apartment, making it seem smaller than ever.

"I didn't expect Bill today; I certainly didn't invite him."

"Did you have dinner with him?"

"It seemed the least I could do. We were good friends."

"Were?"

"He asked me to marry him."

"And?"

"I said no, of course!"

"I don't suppose that did your friendship any good."

"You don't have to sound so damn smug!"

"I didn't realize I was. How long will he be here?"

"He's leaving tomorrow, and I doubt if he'll come back."

"Good."

She wandered into the kitchen area, washing her hands at the sink, trying to pin down the real reason for her agitation.

170

Bill was gone, and he'd been amazingly understanding, everything considered. Alex was hardly flying into a jealous rage, so why was she so angry and defensive? He was blocking her exit from the narrow alcove, hands on his hips, brows arched into a scowl.

"Let me pass."

"Whatever happened to 'How was your day?' or 'I missed you, Alex'?" He didn't move out of her way.

"All right. How was your day?"

"Better than my evening. I did miss you."

"Me the person, or me the warm body?"

She tried to flounce past him, but he captured her between his arms.

"Did Iowa try to tell you I'm some kind of big-city predator, seducing innocent maidens?"

"Nothing like that!" She greatly resented his tone and struggled to get free, not at all mollified when he kissed her soundly, running his hands down her back and fondling her bottom with hard fingers.

"Let me go," she protested.

"So it's good-bye to the liver salesman and don't touch me, Alex?" He did release her.

"Don't be silly. One has nothing to do with the other."

"Did you really have a headache in Connecticut Saturday?"

"No."

"Please don't make up excuses for me. All you have to say is, 'Alex, I don't feel like sleeping with you tonight.' "

"Alex, I don't feel like sleeping with you tonight."

"Or last night or the night before! Did I dream Amsterdam?"

"You know you didn't." She walked to the window, sticking her finger through a hole in the curtain that wasn't part of the lace pattern.

"I don't know what to do about you." The misery in his voice was real.

She bunched the yellowing edge of the curtain into a tight wad, squeezing so hard her fingers ached.

"I have to ask you for time, Katie."

"I don't understand."

"You don't want to." He sat on the couch, staring at the calendar-art painting of a farm.

"You make it sound like I'm trying to pressure you."

"Isn't it enough that we love each other?"

"Have you ever been in love before?" Why did she ask when she didn't want to know the answer?

"I suppose I may have thought so. Nothing like us, Katie, nothing like Amsterdam."

"Maybe you're more of a romantic than you think. Maybe you need candle-lit canal rides and—"

"No!" he said sharply.

"You really don't need me," she said so quietly he barely heard.

"That's not true." He rose and restlessly paced the floor, staying away from the window where she stood, still fingering the curtain.

Her silence frustrated him.

"Is this our first fight?" He forced a tight laugh.

"No, I guess not."

"Good. I'm not very good at handling emotional stuff."

He came up behind her, just standing there while her emotions exploded like popping corn.

"Look at me," he said.

"Not yet." She hugged her arms across her chest.

"When I saw your friend," he said with soft-voiced restraint, "I wanted to wrap the steering wheel around his neck. I wanted to wring yours."

"Then why don't you yell or fight or something?" She turned to face him.

He shrugged his shoulders. "I don't like scenes."

"Scenes! I love scenes! Big, noisy, screaming scenes!" She yanked on the aged curtain, pulling it down, rod and all, and

172

throwing the dusty lace over his head like a gladiator netting an opponent.

"Of all the childish, silly . . ." He ripped at the curtain, sneezing as the dust clogged his nostrils, angrily freeing himself. "What is that supposed to prove?"

"Maybe I want to know if you care enough to shout at me!" she shouted.

Even furious, he kept his voice low and controlled. She wanted to shake some reaction from him, break through his calm, but her outbursts only made him more coldly restrained.

"Maybe this is doing you a world of good, Kate, but it's not my style."

"Of course," she said, "brawling isn't sophisticated! Ripping curtains isn't sophisticated!"

"Maybe we'd better talk about this when you've calmed down."

"I am calm."

It was true; she couldn't sustain her rage in the face of his passive rejection.

"Whatever's bothering you, we can work it out." He sneezed again, his head jerked forward by the force of it.

"At least be angry with me!"

"I am." His eyes were watering from the sneeze, but there was no emotion in his voice. "I'm going, Kate. I'll probably be out of my office most of tomorrow, but we'll straighten all this out after work."

Unbelievably, he left. Deflated as last year's birthday balloon, she didn't even have enough energy left to cry.

Nasty white plaster was showing where she'd pulled the curtain bracket loose, and the yellowing lace was beyond repair. How fortunate that Alex paid her a large enough salary to cover the damage from her tantrum. How terrible that not even her vile temper could penetrate his protective armor. She could forgive him anything: denying her accusation, verbally abusing her foolishness, even making angry

173

love. What she couldn't handle was his icy reserve, his unshakable self-control! Didn't any emotion touch him deeply? Could he love her as passionately as she loved him and still show so little reaction to her anger?

She caught her fingers in the shredded lace, staring at it for a long time, remembering the slow, excruciating path of the feather as it excited her to fantastic heights. Even then Alex had been a model of control, tremendously aroused but fully able to govern his own responses. Was it because he wasn't emotionally committed? Did he slide coolly across the surface of life without ever really getting involved? He ate what he thought was good for him, exercised for his health, went to parties because they were mildly pleasurable and good for business. Did he love the same way—was he satisfied with superficial relationships?

Letting the curtain drop, she knew what she had to do.

CHAPTER TEN

Following through on her decision proved easier than she had anticipated. After a long, sleepless night of activity—she had packed her belongings and restored Linda's wall hangings and knickknacks to their original places—she arrived at the gallery before anyone else. It didn't take long to clear a few personal possessions from her desk and prepare for Blanche a list of appointments to be canceled. Typing her letter of resignation took longer, but after crumpling several attempts, she simply wrote:

To: Alex Gilbert
From: Kate Bevan

With great regret I find it necessary to resign from my position at Gilbert's Antiques Gallery.

She considered adding "Please forgive me," but didn't. Laying the unfolded sheet of paper in his top desk drawer, she hoped it would lie there undiscovered until her plane took off.

Having to pay the rest of the rent on an apartment she couldn't use anymore was annoying, but compared with her other regrets, it was only a pinprick. Giving her key to the superintendent, she left instructions about letting the movers into the apartment and then hurriedly knocked on her neighbor's door, arousing the excited barking of the gray poodle. No other good-byes were necessary; she couldn't say

175

anything to Blanche or Nancy because they were sure to alert Alex.

He probably wouldn't have urged her to stay even if he had known. Avoiding him now was essential only because she wasn't strong enough to leave if she saw him again. She had handled everything efficiently except the pain.

Her anguish grew worse, not better, as the 767 streaked toward Chicago's O'Hare. The connection to Omaha was poor; she had been lucky to get a flight on short notice. Her three-and-a-half-hour wait in the Chicago terminal seemed like that many days when measured by her misery. Alex was everything she wanted in a man: exciting, kind, witty, intelligent. Yet there didn't seem to be a way to stay with him. She couldn't live dangling by her thumbs, torn between the excitement of having a cherished lover and her compelling need for a future with him. She didn't even know if one woman was enough for him. He was a born collector, constantly buying more of his precious stringed instruments. Was novelty in his love life a necessity too? How could she know him so well and still understand so little about him?

A phone call would, of course, bring her parents rushing to meet her at the Omaha airport, but she wasn't ready to see them. She checked into the closest motel and cried herself to sleep, awaking early the next morning to ride a milk-route bus across hot, flat farmland.

Butterfield's one outstanding landmark was the co-op elevator that towered fortresslike over the sprawling community, an oasis surrounded by grainfields. During the winter the snow-buried fields were buffeted by winds that locals swore came straight from the North Pole, and every spring the vast plains turned green again. Kate loved her home state, but was reminded that there was nothing gentle about any of Nebraska's seasons, especially not summer, as she descended from the air-conditioned bus into a furnace of hot wind. The few people moving on the sweltering sidewalks were farmers in overalls and baseball hats or straw headgear, doing necessary business or going to the café where men congregated to complain about the government and compare the progress of their crops.

Walking all the way to the outskirts of town where her parents' home stood was out of the question. They would be alarmed enough by her unexpected arrival without seeing her stagger up to their door suffering from heatstroke.

She fended off her mother's well-intentioned sympathy but told both parents some of the truth over a dinner of sweet corn and T-bones, a combination consolation and homecoming feast.

"I just couldn't work for him feeling the way I do."

"Well, we sure can use you around here," her father said. "Things'll be quiet until after the Fourth, but I've got auctions stacked on auctions right through the fall. Should be the busiest August we've ever had."

"You're not going to put Kate to work the minute she gets home," her mother protested.

"Sure am. Millie Borden's been clerking," he explained to Kate, "but she's having her third in a couple of months. I promised her I'd try to find a temporary replacement until after the baby's born."

"It sounds like just what I need, Dad. Gives me time to decide what I want to do next."

She didn't go to the Fourth of July parade, but the auction house quickly became home again. Most of the summer sales were held in the large corrugated-metal building, which stood a few hundred yards from the family home. Its frayed old theater seats accommodated the bidders, and a clanking air conditioner did not cool the interior enough to make people forget the heat wave outside. In the fall most auctions would be held on farms, whose owners were retiring after one last harvest; but for now the weekly Thursday-night sale was a major source of entertainment for town and country folks. Her father's reputation as a witty auctioneer who got

177

good prices brought him consignments from all over the county and beyond.

Busy didn't mean happy in Kate's case. She set such a feverish pace—checking in consignments, each lot of which had to be numbered and recorded, distributing handbills, talking to potential sellers, and helping with the paperwork necessary to close an auction—that her father complained she wasn't leaving any work for him. She wasn't fooling him a bit.

"Nice fellow, this Alex?" he asked with assumed casualness one afternoon when they were alone in his office.

"Yes," she answered unthinkingly, then realized it was true.

"Only real fault is, he's not yours?" Sam Bevan talked to his daughter the way he did to his friends, and she loved him for it.

"Something like that. I think he cares, but not enough."

"Love's pretty hard to measure," he said sagely, "but I guess he's had enough time to do something about it if he wanted to. I hear the Newman boy is back in town."

"Kenny Newman's no kid! He's over thirty, and if you start matchmaking, Dad, I'll go out on the road."

Show hopping had never pleased her father, although he allowed both his children to find their own way without heavy-handed interference.

"I had no such idea in mind," he said with mock indignation.

Clerking during an auction wasn't as simple as it looked. Kate sat at a high counter beside her mother, who kept one set of sheets while Kate kept the other. They had to record the lot number and name of every item, the selling price, and the bidding number of the buyer. Her father sold at a brisk pace, alternating with another auctioneer who worked with him part-time. Even a small error could cause a big headache, but the Bevan women rarely made one.

The back third of the building was one huge elevated platform with all the merchandise being offered for sale on display behind the auctioneer's podium and the clerk's bench. A crew of at least six men, depending on the size of the sale, watched for bids, carried small merchandise to the winners, and helped with pickups, which could be made at the rear exit behind the platform. The cashier worked through a large window in the office, near the front door of the building. Bidders paid their bills there before claiming large purchases in back, which meant runners continually raced to the cashier with the clerks' sheets. Another helper in the office made out bills for individual bidders.

Enjoying the slight respite from the heat, people came out in droves for the well-advertised estate sale at the auction house, and on this Thursday in early August there was standing room only long before the hour for viewing the merchandise was over. Everything from appliances to a seventy-year accumulation of crocks, garden tools, and furniture was packed on the platform or piled high on tables in front of it. Kate spotted a few antiques dealers and knew they would have a successful evening. There were treasures for everyone in the mass of goods cleaned out of an old frame house in town. It was going to be a very long sale, even at her father's fast pace.

Men with cellars and sheds full of tools bid enthusiastically on old wrenches, hammers, and axes; then mountains of linens, quilts, and throw rugs went to thrifty housewives and a few cagey antiques dealers who knew that fabric art of the past had a great future. Kate bought a lovely old gingham quilt with an unfamiliar pattern that would be fun to research. The buying privilege was never denied to auction workers; the two auctioneers were the only ones in the place who never bid.

Satisfied that she had bought the only item she really wanted, Kate gave her full concentration to her record sheets, looking at the crowd only when an item was knocked down, to be sure she had the correct number from the bid-

179

der's identification card. The runner delivering the merchandise always called it out to the clerks, but Kate also relied on her own powers of observation.

The shock of seeing a dark-haired man edging his way into the room made her reluctant to look again. Since coming home she had been seeing men everywhere who resembled Alex. Why should tonight be different? Given the combination of her imagination and unhappiness, it wasn't surprising that she was seeing things.

"Did you get that price?" her mother asked, jolting Kate to attention.

"Sorry, no." Missing a sale was unforgivable for a clerk, and she sheepishly thanked her mother for giving it to her.

She scanned the crowd again while her father egged on two women who were bidding against each other on a pedal sewing machine with an ornate cast-iron base.

"Don't see machines like this so often anymore," her father urged.

Kate could remember when a bidder could buy one for fifty cents with her father's thanks for hauling it away.

Sighing with relief because she didn't see the dark-haired man again, she recorded the sale and listened with an amused smile while her father suggested uses for a long sticklike gadget with a metal clamp on the end. He could identify ninety-nine percent of his merchandise, but homemade primitives sometimes stumped even him.

When about a third of the estate was sold, her father gave the mike and gavel, but not his cowboy hat, to his associate. After resting his voice, he would call the last part of the auction. Kate liked Jake Bennet, but his spiel was monotonous compared with her father's. Maybe, if she stayed home long enough, she would go to auctioneers' school. She already knew how to call an auction, and what better place to apprentice than in her father's business? It was one part of the antiques trade she hadn't tried.

Planning anything for the future always threw a damper

on her mood, not that she was jovial on her best days. She wanted to be with Alex more than she wanted to breathe; the way she constantly imagined seeing him was proof of that. Yet, their differences would still be there if she did see him again. She loved him far too much to endure a short-lived, lukewarm affair.

Spectators who arrived too late to secure an old theater seat stood in bunches along the back and side walls, moving about frequently, patronizing the snack bar, going outside for a smoke, and returning with the hope that a seat had been vacated. The standing crowd did bid, but most of the sales were made to the more attentive seated people who had come early enough to examine the merchandise. Serious buyers rarely arrived late. A farmer leaning against the north wall did make the high bid on a lot of old hay hooks, and Kate looked in his direction to confirm his number after the auctioneer said, "Sold to one hundred twenty-seven." *Alex* was standing beside the successful bidder!

The pen stayed in her hand, but she couldn't do anything with it. This time her eyes weren't playing tricks. Alex met her startled gaze, moving his lips into that crazy half-grin, challenging her in a way she didn't understand.

"Kate!"

The urgency in her mother's voice forced her to make a notation of the farmer's bid, but it didn't steady her hand or stop the pounding of her heart. Fortunately, two bidders were hesitantly vying for a wicker plant stand, giving her a few instants to breathe deeply and try to calm down. When she looked up again to record the winner's number, the spot where Alex had stood was empty.

She was imagining things! Biting the end of her pen in agitation, she wondered if her brain was going soft, conjuring up counterfeit copies of Alex because she wanted the real man so badly. Kate had been perched on the stool, poised over the record sheets, for over four hours, and her legs and back longed for a good stretch. The crowd had thinned a little, but not a great deal, since bargains often came in the last minutes of the sale when many had spent their limit. Her father was cleaning up some box lots from the garage of the estate, the kind of clutter no one needed. It went mostly to people who wanted to spend a dollar in hopes of finding some valuable item lost in a box of otherwise useless junk.

"Well, that does it, folks," Sam Bevan said at last. "Don't forget, we've got a nice 1972 Plymouth at next Thursday's sale. Best condition I've seen in a long time. Also there's a—"

"I'd like to bid on one more lot tonight," a loud voice interrupted.

Kate had never been so aware of Alex's eastern accent as she was that moment in her father's auction house. Alex had everyone's attention; even the cashier in the front office forgot about collecting from the line of bidders waiting to pay.

"We've sold everything in the estate," her father said, never in the least bit ruffled by anything a spectator did.

"I want to buy time, your clerk's time," Alex said quickly.

"Son, Nebraska never was a slave state." He got a few laughs with that, but the audience was waiting avidly to see what would happen.

"I'll open the bidding at fifty dollars for a half hour of conversation with Kate," Alex persisted.

Her father looked at her, seemed about to refuse, then changed his mind.

"Dad!" Kate tried frantically to catch his eye, aware of the amused hush in the still-crowded room. She couldn't believe what was happening!

"I bid fifty-five," a rumbling bass voice chimed in.

"Sixty," shouted a farmer Kate recognized, a longtime friend of her family's.

"I have sixty, do I hear sixty-five, sixty-five . . ."

Alex signaled sixty-five with his bidding card.

"Seventy," the first voice yelled.

The crowd was in on the fun now, laughing and calling

182

encouragement as several more local men joined the contest, none of them worrying at all that the easterner would drop out and stick them with the bid.

Kate had to explain to her mother what was happening, doing so in a few desperately whispered sentences. She wanted to shrink to the size of a mouse and creep away under the platform; there was no other way to leave without running the gauntlet of laughing auction-goers in front or ribald employees in back of her. How could Alex do this to her!

"Ninety-five, who'll make it a hundred?" Her father sounded as amused as everyone else!

"A hundred," Alex said firmly.

"Sold!" Sam Bevan knew when to cut off a joke. When one of the other bidders protested, he said, "Now, Harry, Eunice would skin you alive if you won this lot."

Kate refused to look in Alex's direction. Her face felt as if the heat wave had returned, and she was furious with her father too. If this was his way of playing Cupid, he'd better turn in his bow and arrow. She knew the man who approached the counter was Alex, even though only the top of his head showed above the level of the writing surface.

"Can I claim my lot here?" he asked.

"Nothing leaves the platform without a receipt," she said coldly.

By the time he stood in line to pay for his ridiculous bid, she would be far out of reach.

Her mother started to say something, then, uncharacteristically, decided against it. Kate pulled the quilt she had bought from under the counter, and stood to leave, then watched in stunned dismay while all the successful bidders waiting to pay their bills moved back a few steps, making room for Alex at the head of the line. The cashier took his cash and handed him a receipt in the quickest exchange ever made in the auction house. The whole town was conspiring against her! She hurried to the rear exit, only to find it blocked by two of her father's stockiest helpers who were carrying out a large but fragile china cabinet with maddening slowness. Her father was pretending to be totally absorbed in conversation with a few regulars, keeping his back to his daughter.

"My receipt." Alex showed it to her with grim seriousness.

"You didn't have to put on that charade! You could've asked me if I wanted to talk to you!"

"You might have told me you were leaving New York! How do you think I felt when Blanche found your resignation in my desk after I'd tried all night to locate you?"

"Blanche found it?" She felt a little sick.

"She needed my key for the file."

"I'm sorry about that."

"Only that?"

"This is my mother," Kate said, nodding at her innocent but curious parent who had just approached them.

"Mrs. Bevan, I'm Alex Gilbert." He shook her hand and politely excused both of them.

"I'm not going anywhere with you!"

He took her arm none too gently and propelled her toward the rear exit and out onto the loading dock. The bustle of checking out and loading merchandise stopped, all eyes turning to her. But Kate was darned if she would provide any more entertainment. She walked rapidly down the six wooden steps to the ground and passed a lineup of waiting vans and trucks, out of the lighted area.

"Over here," Alex said curtly, not touching her again. He stopped beside the dark hulk of a farm truck and opened the door on the passenger side.

"What are you doing with this?"

"Renting it."

"Why?" She couldn't have been more surprised if he had ushered her into a hot-air balloon.

"Get in."

184

"For thirty minutes of conversation," she warned.

"That's what I paid for."

Alex seemed as out of place in the old truck as she'd once felt at Myra Webster's apartment. The seats were patched with strips of plastic tape, and the floor mat by her feet was a ragged scrap of rubber. He managed to back up and negotiate a path through the departing crowd, but not without a few choice words for the unfamiliar floor shift. She realized she was still clutching the quilt under one arm, then wadded it more tightly and hugged it against her.

"Where are we going?"

"I found some deserted property this afternoon with a grove of trees. I was beginning to believe this state was one big grainfield."

"No one invited you here. You have twenty-three minutes left."

"I have thirty. Our conversation hasn't started yet."

Why couldn't her father have invited him home like a normal parent instead of going along with his silly bidding? She could hear the rapid pounding of her heart.

She knew where they were headed; young kids regularly cruised the countryside searching out secluded parking spots, and she had had her share of social life in high school. Alex left the paved county road, followed a gravel road past several farms, and ended up on a rutted dirt lane that threatened to shake the truck into a heap of loose parts.

"Isn't this a little extreme?" she asked caustically.

"No one will hear us shouting here."

"Is that what we're going to do?"

"I am."

The grove was little more than a clump of straggly bushes, but the solitude was unnerving when he cut the motor and turned off the headlights.

"This is hardly your kind of place," she said.

"What do you know about my kind of anything?"

185

"Nothing." She clamped her jaws together; if he wanted a conversation, he could do the talking.

He left the truck, closing the metal door with a thud and walking to her side.

"I'd rather stay in here."

"Get out."

"For someone who should be arrested, you have some nerve giving me orders."

"Arrested for what?"

"Kidnapping!"

"You came willingly!"

"I certainly did not! I just didn't want another idiotic scene."

"You like scenes when you stage them."

"Not with hundreds of people watching."

"Hardly hundreds."

"You humiliated me in front of a lot of people I know."

"So you chose to come with me instead of making a fuss? Out!" His voice was so angry it was hardly recognizable.

"Your time has started," she said stiffly, laying aside the quilt and sliding off the seat, right into his arms.

His hands circled her throat, and his thumbs caressed soft hollows between the tendons. His kiss was angry and hurtful, but she dug her fingers into his shoulders in response, feeling an explosiveness that was a blend of fury, hurt, and longing.

"That isn't conversation," she whispered, grasping at her own shattered pride.

"Neither is this."

He kissed her again, deeply, more tenderly but no less passionately, crushing her body against his.

"Why did you leave?" he asked quietly as he released her.

"I didn't want to be your mistress!"

"You weren't!"

"What would you call it?"

186

"Being in love, but maybe I was the only one who felt that way."

She turned from him and made her way in the moonlight to the back of the truck, then leaned her forehead on the edge of the high tailgate.

"Do you love me?" he asked urgently.

"Yes." She couldn't look at him.

"Do you believe I love you?" He put his arms around her then, his groin hard against her backside.

"I did in Amsterdam, but it was a fairy tale. Nothing so wonderful lasts."

"You didn't give it a chance." He nuzzled her neck and sighed.

"I've been home a long time."

"Ages."

"You didn't call or write or anything."

"Do you want me to admit how much you hurt my pride? Katie, I thought you were the woman I'd been looking for most of my life, and then you left."

"How could I stay not knowing whether your love was going to last?"

"Damn it, Kate, life doesn't come with written guarantees! Don't you think what we had going deserved a little time? I couldn't rethink my whole life in a few weeks."

"How could I know you were rethinking anything? Where I come from, people fall in love and get married!"

"And buy homes in the suburbs and have a flock of kids!"

"Well, a couple anyway. This isn't getting us anywhere! Your thirty minutes must be up."

"We'll stay for thirty days, if that's what it takes!"

"What takes?"

"I've been in hell since you left!" He ran his hands down her back, circling her waist and pressing closer.

"I can't talk when you're crushing me," she said breathlessly.

"Do you want to talk?" His mouth opened over hers,

187

feasting on soft lips and spearing her pliant tongue with his until she clutched at him.

"No," she moaned, feeling drugged by the sudden rush of emotions after the long arid days without him.

"Nice of you to bring a blanket," he teased, sounding more like the man she loved.

"I didn't bring it! I just forgot to leave it behind."

He opened the tailgate. "Climb up." But he didn't give her a chance; he draped the quilt over his shoulder and circled her waist with his hands, then slowly ran them up her sides until his thumbs stroked the undersides of her breasts.

She covered his hands, her fingers riding on his while he caressed the soft mounds imprisoned in cloth; he kissed her with growing urgency. Throwing the quilt in the back of the truck, he slowly took her in his arms again, letting her feel his warm breath on her eyelids and tickling her upper lip with his.

"I love you, Katie."

"I love you so much!"

Her blue plaid auction-night blouse parted under his fingers, and her jeans fell to a tangle around her feet, sending up dust from the beaten weeds when she stepped free.

"Let's get in the truck," he said hoarsely, breaking a bra strap in his haste to snatch away the garment and then taking the weight of her breasts in his hands, bending to kiss each in turn.

"I can't believe this is real," she murmured, confused by happiness and longing.

"What we have is real, darling, and it's going to go on and on and on until you wonder what you ever saw in a doddering old fool like me."

Joyfully convinced because she wanted to be, she slid his shirt over his rib cage. Her palms made a slow circle over his nipples; her fingers ran through silky damp hair when he raised his arms to help her. His tailored slacks joined her jeans in a billow of dust. After spreading out the quilt over the straw, he lifted her onto the back of the truck and lay down beside her.

His breath was warm, and he covered her face and breasts with heated, impulsive kisses, leaning over her like a marble Adonis in the moonlight, the lines of his body firm and smooth. Alex kneaded her skin from shoulders to ankles as she lay on the soft quilted cotton, his touch an intimate torture, until she gathered him into her arms for an unbearably sweet exchange of kisses. His warm mouth covered her breasts, teasing each peak to tautness, and then unable to restrain himself any longer, he frantically plunged between her thighs, his raw urgency driving her into a mindless frenzy.

The stars overhead were pale darts of light compared with the explosion of pleasure that skyrocketed through her consciousness, and she welcomed his collapsing weight, wanting to melt into one being.

With a soft laugh he rolled to her side, rubbing his hands over his eyes. "Now I'm the one who thinks this is too good to be real."

"Your thirty minutes are up," she teased, recapturing one of his hands and holding it against her.

"No, this isn't what I paid for."

"It certainly isn't!"

"No more games. When do you want to get married?" he asked.

"To whom?" His leg was heavy across hers, but it only tempted her to wiggle closer.

"There's only one candidate." He held her face between his hands, kissing her soundly.

"I've had other offers."

"I know. You dangled one in front of me obviously enough."

"I did no such thing!" She struggled but couldn't break free. "I never—"

189

His kisses interrupted, telling her how little anything but her answer mattered.

Loving him so much she was crying with happiness, she brushed a tear making a wet path on her face. "I must be allergic to straw."

"You're not allergic to anything! Katie, my life is empty without you. Are you going to marry me?"

"Yes, I am," she replied fervently, and then added on a lighter note, "Can I have my job back too?"

"You could have it back without marrying me. I'm in love, but I'm not loony." He entwined her fingers in his, bringing one knuckle to his lips to be kissed.

"I love you, Alex." She leaned toward him, rubbing her nose against his.

"You can't wear off your freckles that way," he teased softly.

His shoulder was slippery under her cheek, and she tingled when he traced the outline of her ear with one fingertip. The stillness was broken only by the barely audible whispers of nature's night life.

"Let's make plans," she said, holding his hand and exploring the hollows between his fingers.

"We'll get a license tomorrow and get married as soon as the law allows," he said.

"I think I want a small wedding. Just relatives and close friends."

"How many close friends?" He brought her wrist to his lips, kissing the sensitive inner side.

"Oh, a hundred or so." He was making it difficult to think straight.

"You can't plan a wedding of that size in three days."

"I was thinking of a Christmas wedding, red velvet gowns for the bridesmaids—"

"Christmas! When I win a bid I take possession immediately."

"Does this mean you're adding me to your collection?"

190

she asked with mock indignation, rising to her knees and studying his face, resting her hands on his shoulders.

"It means," he said slowly, pulling her into his arms, "that I've found the answer to every collector's dream: a one of a kind, priceless treasure that will keep me happy for the rest of my life."

Now you can reserve February's
Candlelights
<u>before</u> they're published!

- 💜 You'll have copies set aside for *you* the instant they come off press.
- 💜 You'll save yourself precious shopping time by arranging for *home delivery.*
- 💜 You'll feel proud and efficient about organizing a system that *guarantees* delivery.
- 💜 You'll avoid the disappointment of not finding *every* title you want and need.

ECSTASY SUPREMES $2.50 each

- ☐ 61 **FROM THIS DAY FORWARD,** Jackie Black 12740-8-27
- ☐ 62 **BOSS LADY,** Blair Cameron 10763-6-31
- ☐ 63 **CAUGHT IN THE MIDDLE,** Lily Dayton 11129-3-20
- ☐ 64 **BEHIND THE SCENES,** Josephine Charlton Hauber 10419-X-88

ECSTASY ROMANCES $1.95 each

- ☐ 306 **ANOTHER SUNNY DAY,** Kathy Clark.................10202-2-30
- ☐ 307 **OFF LIMITS,** Sheila Paulos 16568-7-27
- ☐ 308 **THRILL OF THE CHASE,** Donna Kimel Vitek.......18662-5-10
- ☐ 309 **DELICATE DIMENSIONS,** Dorothy Ann Bernard 11775-5-35
- ☐ 310 **HONEYMOON,** Anna Hudson.............................13772-1-18
- ☐ 311 **LOST LETTERS,** Carol Norris 14984-3-10
- ☐ 312 **APPLE OF MY EYE,** Carla Neggers 10283-9-24
- ☐ 313 **PRIDE AND JOY,** Cathie Linz 16935-6-23